THE
BELLTREES
INCIDENT
DECEPTION

Elizabeth Munton

THE BELLTREES INCIDENT

Copyright

Text copyright © Elizabeth Munton, 2020

Cover design by Grzegorz Japoł, book-cover.design

Disclaimer

Acknowledgements

For my Mum, whom had little schooling helped me create stories and always listened with enthusiasm.

For Kathy, Margaret, Melinda, Rebecca, Graham and retired NSW Police Officers John and Geoff thank you all for helping me during this journey.

CHAPTER

1

Bronwyn and Ryan Prior sat at their dining table, mouths gagged, hands tied behind their backs. A tear rolled down Bronwyn's cheek. The music that had been playing on the radio behind them suddenly stopped. Bronwyn's eyes darted anxiously from right to left looking at the two masked men standing in front of them. Trying not to heave, Ryan felt his heart racing as the cold hard muzzle of the gun was pressed into the side of his face.

With a grin on his face the taller man said, "I'm Benno. We're going to play a little game of chance. I'm going to ask you some questions, and for every wrong answer my friend here will break one of your wife's toes."

They both looked at the second man. Pointing to him he said, "he's mute. He only answers to me, right big man?"

Tilting his head from side to side, the second man grunted as if in agreeance.

Removing Ryan's mouth gag Benno said, "let's begin. ... Oh, I forgot to mention there are only three questions!"

"Do anything to me, but please, please let my wife go! I'm begging you". Ryan's words came out as a sob.

"Where are you hiding my shipment?" Benno asked, completely ignoring Ryan.

"I don't know who you are, and I don't know what you are talking about!" he replied.

Benno slammed his hand down on the table. "Wrong answer! Gav go start your work on toe number one".

Gav roughly grabbed Bronwyn's right foot, and pulled the big toe, twisting it in a complete circle.

Bronwyn screamed a muffled scream, pain etched on her face as she struggled in vain.

Ryan turned his head towards his wife. Once again, he felt the cold muzzle of the gun dig deeper into the side of his face.

"Who are you working for?"

"I honestly don't know what you are talking about!" Ryan screamed.

"Wrong answer again! Gav start toe number two," Benno ordered.

Knowing what was coming, Bronwyn didn't wait but instead, kicked Gav hard in the groin using her other foot.

The result of her effort forced the chair to collapse, legs splintering under her, tipping the chair over. The ropes that had bound her hands so tightly now lay loosely coiled on the floor.

A beeping sound informed Benno that he had received a text message. He took the mobile from his pocket and read the text. His demeanour immediately changed.

Putting the phone to his ear, he said, "wrong number! You're telling me it's the wrong number?" "Well folks, it's your lucky day. Our little game of chance is over."

Benno viciously struck Ryan across the back of the head with his pistol, rendering him unconsciousness. He kicked the chair and it landed sideways on the floor. "C'mon big man, we're done here."

Bronwyn watched him tilt his head slightly from side to side but this time there was no grunting. As he fiddled with his mask it dropped down, allowing her to have a brief visual of his face as he walked past her and out the door.

"Oh, shit it hurts" she moaned as she dragged herself across the floor towards her husband. "Ryan honey, please wake up," she urged gently rubbing her hand across his chest.

A blue flashing light in his pocket caught her attention. "Yes, your mobile." She pulled the phone vigorously from his pocket and dialling 000.

"Police, Fire or Ambulance?" the radio operator asked.

"Police and Ambulance," Bronwyn replied.

"What state and suburb are you calling from?" the operator asked.

"NSW, Northbridge." Bronwyn could hear the hollow ring tone as the operator asked her to stay on the line. Before long the call was connected.

"Northbridge Police," a female voice announced.

"My name is Bronwyn Prior. I live at 37 Pringle Street, Northbridge. Two masked men have forced their way into our home. My husband is badly hurt, please come quickly."

"Police and Ambulance have been despatched; they will be there shortly. Please remain calm Bronwyn. I'm Constable Vickers and I will stay on the phone with you until they arrive. Are you injured?"

"Yes, but I'm ok. My husband is unconscious. He was struck on the back of the head with a gun, he has a deep cut which is bleeding," Bronwyn continued anxiously.

Bronwyn cried a sigh of relief as she heard the approaching sirens. She told the officer that both Police and Ambulance had arrived and thanked the police and ambulance officers as they entered the house to assist.

A young ambulance officer approached Bronwyn, "my name is Vanessa, I can see you have an injured foot, are you hurt anywhere else?"

"No! I'm ok. Please, ...please help my husband." She gestured towards the unconscious figure lying motionless on the floor.

Placing a chair next to Bronwyn Vanessa said, "my partner will help your husband. Let's sit you on the chair so we can take a look at that foot".

Crouching down next to Bronwyn a male police officer said, "Bronwyn I'm Constable Peters. Can you tell me what exactly happened here tonight?"

"Ryan, my husband answered a knock at the door. Two men wearing facemasks forced their way into the house. One man pointed a gun at Ryan's head as he pushed him inside. The second man followed behind" describing the evenings events as best she could remember.

"Did you recognise his voice, Bronwyn?" he asked.

"No and we sure as hell didn't know what he was talking about" she replied sobbing as she spoke.

"Try and stay calm. You're doing really well Bronwyn" he continued.

"I remember something, the man with the gun called someone. Whatever that person said to him made him angry. He responded by yelling wrong street number!" she continued between gasps.

 The ambulance officer assisted Bronwyn gently into the ambulance. Just before the doors closed, she called out to the police officer and said, "Constable, he told us the second man was mute. It was weird, he grunted and tilted his head from side to side. Oh, the man that had the gun called him Gav. Also, the mute man dropped his mask. I think it is behind the front door."

Spotting the mask laying behind the front door and using the end of her pen, Constable Peters placed the mask in an evidence bag.

"Thank you, Bronwyn. The Detectives may want to speak with you in the hospital. Please let them know if you remember anything else" he said.

CHAPTER

2

"Good afternoon, I'm Fiona Forrester, coming to you live from News Central Radio 101. Welcome to Midday!

"Beautiful day outside but sadly it won't last. Southerly change arriving late this afternoon. Top temperature for both Sydney and the western suburbs will be in the low 30's before the southerly which is expected to arrive around 4pm.

"School holidays are over, and kids are back in the classroom. How do you feel about that? My house is very quiet, perhaps a little too quiet. Nina Shelley avid cat lover will be dropping in this afternoon. Nina will also be bringing her rescue cat Khaleesi into the studio. I've seen photos, but I can't wait to meet her.

Wil Marks our chef is dropping in this afternoon, and he tells me has cooked up a treat. Details will be posted on the website.

"But first I want to start with the home invasion last night. What a terrifying experience that would have been for the Northbridge couple.

Channel 9 news reporter Lee Baker is on the line with an update on the Northbridge home invasion.

"Hi Lee. The Police are calling the home invasion at Northbridge last night a case of mistaken identity."

"Yes Fiona, Police have confirmed two armed masked men forced their way into the Northbridge home and held the occupant's captive. The terrifying experience lasted for about an hour. Police have also confirmed the intruders assaulted the couple. The male occupant of the house has a head injury while the female has a foot injury. Both are in a stable condition in hospital. There is an ongoing investigation into the incident. One line of enquiry Police are checking is looking into CCTV cameras installed in homes in Pringle Street. While the police have reported the Northbridge home invasion last night as a case of mistaken identity, they have not ruled out whether this was a gang or drug related incident.

"Thank you, Lee.

"Nina Shelley, avid cat lover has just walked into the studio and has brought with her rescue cat Khaleesi. I'm going to describe what I am seeing right now. Nina has just opened the cat carrier. If Khaleesi could talk. The look on her face is priceless - why did you wake me up Mum? Cat cuteness overload right now! Nina, what made you decide on a rescue cat?"

"I grew up with a cat named Ginger. When she died at sixteen years old I was devastated. A friend who was going through a difficult time asked if I could look after her cat Zoe until things settled down. I was hesitant at first, but you know Zoe was great company for me.

"I was disappointed after 3-4 months that I had to hand Zoe back. My home was so quiet. My friend suggested we go to the RSPCA, just to look. There were so many beautiful kittens, but I had already decided if I was going to get another cat, I would get an older one. Cats over ten years old are called senior cats. At the very end of the senior's row, I saw a beautiful cat. I asked if I could have a cuddle, and when I picked her up I just knew she was mine. Without thinking I blurted out yes, I'll take her. I named her Khaleesi."

"So, Nina for anyone out there that may be thinking of getting a cat, would you suggest going to a breeder or getting a rescue cat?"

"Think about a rescue cat. They need a home, to feel loved and a lot more too. It saddens me for the cats that are kept purely for breeding. I love Khaleesi. She brings so much joy to my life, and I wouldn't have it any other way."

"Chef Wil Marks has just entered the studio, followed by my staff who are posing as bodyguards protecting the enticing smell of one of his gourmet woodfire pizzas.

"Wil, I bet when you woke up this morning you didn't think that your pizza would cause such a stir. Tell me, why are your pizzas so popular?"

"Fiona, no I certainly didn't. The super supreme pizza is my father's recipe which I swore to secrecy never to reveal the base ingredients. It is the most popular pizza on our menu."

"Whether you have a special cat story you want to share with us or talk about your favourite pizza, give me a call now on 131101."

CHAPTER

3

Natalie stood in the doorway leaning against the door of her small slightly rundown Liverpool house as she looked at PK and said, "well look what the cat left at my door!"

"Now, that's no way to greet me!" PK snapped.

"What do you want PK?" she asked.

"You going to invite me in or what?"

Natalie stood aside and gestured that PK enter her house. PK started raving about a gig he had been invited to.

"You come to gloat, don't bother!"

"I'd take you, but the boss hasn't forgiven you after you cheated him out of his share of a job last year."

"Come on PK. You know I've got my act together" she replied nudging his arm.

"Ok already! "I'll phone him, but I can't guarantee he'll say yes."

PK looked at Nat, dialled his own mobile number, waited a moment and then said, "voice mail! Hey, mate I'm at Nat's house. Ok if I bring Nat along to the gig? Call me back."

"We're not going to wait for an answer. Give me a few minutes to freshen up and I'll meet you at your car" Nat said.

Stepping into PK's car a few minutes later, she asked, "well did he get back to you?"

Lying he said, "yeah, yeah, it's all good."

After what seemed like an eternity, they arrived at the luxurious Belrose house. Natalie observed the beautifully landscaped front garden and assortment of flowering plants. It wasn't until she saw the Mercedes convertible in the driveway that she raised her eyebrows and mumbled to herself, *Wow* you have done *well*!

Her jealousy was obvious as she pressed the doorbell and David opened the door wearing a sporty polo shirt and tailored trousers. He squinted in the daylight as he asked, "hey PK, what are you doing here?"

"Well, look at you in your rich fit clothes!" Nat said.

Looking directly at PK he asked, "mate, what are you doing?"

Slapping PK on the shoulder Nat yelled, "you didn't get a reply from Stephen, did you?"

In annoyance she walked right past PK and David and began surveying the lounge room. Teasing him she picked up a crystal vase and said, "you certainly have done ok for yourself David!"

Looking up to the ceiling in annoyance David said, "this isn't my house. Don't go touching anything."

"My old man left me and I'm running short of cash. Do you have a job I can do for you? PK knows I am good for it!" Nat said.

"Yeah, like the last time. Your job was simple. Deliver a package. But you stole from me Nat. How can I trust you?" PK asked.

David muttered, "you had simple instructions PK, keep an eye on her."

"It's not PK's fault David. I may have invited myself" she said.

Nat decided to explore the downstairs part of the house. She began walking away from David and PK, but something made her stop in her tracks. Her heart started racing, and her face went clammy. She walked back into the lounge room and David saw her shocked face, but more alarming he saw that she was playing with her fingers something he had noticed she did only when nervous.

"Who is that?" she asked.

David crossed the room and grabbed Natalie's arm. Using a tissue, he pushed a card into the lining of her left sleeve. "You didn't see anything, and you can't be here, it's too dangerous. Time for you to leave."

Being so caught up with Nat, David was unaware that Stephen had entered the house.

"What the hell is this! Who is that woman standing in my lounge room?"

"Sorry boss, I brought her here," PK said.

"If you pull a stunt like this again, I'm coming for you. Get her out of my house now PK."

When they were alone, Stephen turned to David. "This cannot happen again. Do you hear me?"

He pulled a mobile out from his pocket and listened to his voice messages. Beckoning David with his hand, he said, "get the guns, we have a problem!"

CHAPTER

4

It was just before midday when Robert's mobile phone rang. Answering, he was surprised when the caller announced his name.

"It's Brian Allan."

"Fuck man! I had no idea where you went."

"Shut up and listen! I'm only allowed to make one phone call a week, so pay attention."

"Last week I posted you a letter. Read it carefully so you understand exactly what I have asked you to do. Do you understand?"

"Yes, I understand," Robert replied.

"Reliable intel advised me that Henry is meeting with business clients at the old warehouse next week. If the intel is correct, there could be an auction. You need to be there but make a low-key appearance. We can't afford any red flags" Brian said. "Make a booking to visit me in a couple of weeks, you can then give me an update."

"Ok, will do." Robert hurriedly replied before slamming down the phone and rushing out to check his letter box.

Sifting through his mail, he began disposing of the junk when he came across a letter addressed to Trish. Checking the back of the envelope he saw the return address and knew this was from Brian.

Carefully opening the envelope, he began reading the short letter, specifically reading one sentence over and over.

Talking out loud he said, "Hi Trish, check in on Henrietta and tell me how the kids are going."

Reading it over and over, he finally understood his instructions.

Robert knew immediately what was happening, with rapid pounding of his heart, shortness of breath, and sweaty palms. A panic attached. *Fuck! I don't think I can do this.* He drummed his fingers on the desk before pressing the contact icon.

Wiping his hands up and down his trouser legs, he scrolled down to H, and clicked on Henry. Moving his eyes further down the contact details he saw the word HOME and a map beside the address. Clicking the screen once, the map opened, and a red dot identified the location of the address.

After regaining his composure, he said to himself, "you can do this", as he checked the time, picked up his binoculars and car keys and left his house.

The road came to an end as he neared the location. Surveying the surrounding area, a high brick fence and CCTV cameras provided a degree of complete privacy with no sightline to the massive property nestled behind it.

Stopping the car under a low canopy of tree branches he placed his phone in his top pocket and picked up his binoculars by the neck strap, before slowly climbing higher up the tree in the hope of a clearer view over the brick fence.

Once settled, he began adjusting the binoculars to get a clearer view.

Aghast by what he saw, he retrieved his phone from his pocket and began taking photos. Opening notes, he tapped the microphone button and dictated the text to ensure he described every detail of what lay behind the fence of secrecy.

"Very private property with CCTV cameras positioned around it. There is one large building which looks like the living quarters. From the view I have, the building has wrought iron door grills. On the eastern side of the property there are approximately four small free-standing buildings with intersecting pathways, large sliding doors and windows that open out to an enclosed yard. Each yard has its own obstacle course."

Someone had spotted him hiding in the tree. Quickly climbing down, he fell on the car before rolling off and onto the ground. Scrambling up, he opened the door, he quickly drove away. *Shit, that was a little too close for comfort!*

It was nearly midnight when his mobile beeped indicating he had received a text message. Not recognising the number, he hesitated for a few minutes before opening the message.

Use this number to send me texts, BA

CHAPTER

5

Driving away from Stephen's house PK asked Natalie, "what were you and David talking about?"

"He told me I wasn't invited and should leave."

"Did he say anything else?"

"Nope! You can drop me off at Central, I'll make my own way home."

He waved a bag of weed at her. "Look what I have, let's go have some fun!"

"Not interested." She pulled the passenger door lever only to see it was locked. "Arsehole! Let me out. Unlock the door PK I want to get out."

In a fit of rage PK slammed her head on the dash so hard that she lost consciousness. Her body fell limp. Blood smeared the window.

Nightfall was nearing. Having grown up in Frenchs Forest, PK knew a few places where he could dispose of her. Driving along Wakehurst Parkway he found an area with overgrown trees near the golf club.

Natalie was beginning to stir. Panicking he hit her again and she slipped back into unconsciousness. *Why did you make me do that Nat?*

Thinking as he tapped the steering wheel PK suddenly had an idea.

"Aah there you are" he mumbled to himself as he tugged at a pair of gloves and length of rope out from behind the front passenger seat and placed both on the floor between his feet.

Looking in the rear-view mirror again, PK thought he was being followed. Pulling over to the left he watched a four-wheel drive pass him and continue down the road.

He pulled into a small open area and decided he was far enough from the main road. His mobile vibrated in his pocket, alerting him of an incoming call.

Eyes flashing open Natalie gasped for air. She was in a car surrounded by blackness. From somewhere behind her she could hear a voice. She touched her forehead. It was sore and wet. A white light lit up the sky for a few moments, enough time for her to realise her hands were covered in blood.

She felt confused as she sat up and struggled to work out where she was. Another flash of light showed her she was surrounded by trees.

Where the hell am I?

She listened closer to the voice. She could tell it was PK. She pictured that he was standing behind the car.

"Yeah, just left Nat tucked away in her house."

She shook her head in disbelief. She carefully opened the door and slowly slid to her feet. Still experiencing discomfort, she finally managed to gain her balance before taking a chance to escape.

She stumbled, tripping over her own feet and stopped to listen, wondering if he was still on the phone.

Then instinct took over. She started running aimlessly, her entire body aching from pain.

The muscles in her legs began to tire. The moon was visible in the sky, allowing her a glimpse of her location. It also allowing her to check whether she was being followed.

Trembling, she fumbled for the phone in her pocket. Clicking contacts, she scrolled down until she found David's name. Opening his details, she clicked again hearing the ring tone.

"Pick up. Come on David pick up," she pleaded under her breath.

It went straight to voicemail. "David, I'm scared. PK attacked me. I passed out and when I woke, I found that we were parked in bushland. I heard him talking to you on the phone. I'm hiding in the scrub." She paused for a moment to listen.

"Someone is coming," she whispered quickly ending the phone call and pushing the phone into her back pocket.

"There you are Nat! Why did you run girl?"

He tied the rope around her hands and dragged her back in the direction of the car. He propped her up against a tree, her phone falling out of her pocket and landing behind her.

"You understand I can't leave any loose ends!"

"Help!" she yelled.

He was unaware that Natalie had already left a voice message for David as he stamped his heel on the phone, crushing it into the wet earth.

Screwing a silencer onto the barrel of a gun he pointed the weapon at Natalie. With a smile on his face, he pulled the trigger twice. One bullet slammed into Natalie's head, the second hitting a nearby tree. Moving her body slightly into position, he placed a package of dope beside her body.

Drug deal gone wrong, he thought as he walked away.

CHAPTER

6

PK was busy watching the motorbike racing when his phone rang.

Before he had a chance to speak Benjamin said, "meet me at 10pm tonight. I'll text you the address."

Arriving at the address, he approached the front entrance of the old, dilapidated warehouse. He could hear the sound of cheering coming from somewhere within. Using face recognition, a security guard scanned PK's face before escorting him inside to the rear of the building.

"Over here," Benjamin said beckoning him to the corner of the room.

Offering him a beer he said, "welcome!"

"Cheers!" PK replied. "What's this place?"

"Henry bought this warehouse when he created his sophisticated elite group and invited certain organisations to invest money. Here you will see a group of AIs going under the hammer. Think of it as an auction, the highest bidder wins."

"You're auctioning them off?"

A tall man, looking like a CEO and dressed in a core-coloured suit, reached out to shake Benjamin's hand. "I'm Robert. Henry invited me."

"Benjamin White!"

PK turned his head to face Robert and said, "don't look so worried. This is a game for Benjamin. It's business. You have to think like him."

Benjamin rubbed his hands together and said, "I hear you're going to make a bid on my entrants tonight."

"You mean Henry's entrants!"

Benjamin gave a long-exaggerated sigh and stormed off towards the bar. Phoning Henry he said, "thought I would let you know Robert showed up tonight."

"He declined. Check your phone, just sent through his photo."

"That isn't the man standing with PK at the bar right now."

"PK! I told you he can't be trusted. Why would you risk everything involving that loser? Call it off immediately!" Henry yelled before slamming down the phone.

Benjamin whistled loudly to catch the attention of everyone in the room. "I am sorry to advise you that this evening's event has been cancelled. Security will see everyone out. Robert you're with me."

"Where are we going?" he asked.

"Thought you and I could have a private event. First things first, you have the cash?"

Cash? I prefer to do a wire transfer."

Robert struggled for a few moments before realising his cover was blown. "When did you realise?"

With a probing finger Benjamin yelled aggressively, "well you see my friend, I didn't until just now!" Still maintaining eye contact Benjamin softly slapped the side of Robert's face. "You're in deep shit, the night is not ending as you planned!"

Tapping PK on the shoulder he said, "I'll leave you to get rid of this piece of shit!"

"No! No! Please, I won't tell anyone about your operation."

Ignoring Robert's pleas, Benjamin sarcastically asked, "what size shoes do you wear, 9 or 10?" Replying to his own question he said, "I think size 10, don't you?" He chuckled quietly to himself.

Waiting until Benjamin had left the premises PK said, "you idiot! Brian suggested you make a *low-key* appearance.

You do know what that means, don't you? Are you that brainless? Do you want to end up at the bottom of the river wearing cement shoes?"

"Security is still outside. So, with that said, I must rough you up a bit." He punched Robert in the face a few times before dragging him out the back of the warehouse and throwing him into the van.

CHAPTER

7

Using the number that Brian Allan gave him, Robert Burns sent a text *'booked in to visit you this Saturday 10am.'*

Brian Allan replied saying he was looking forward to the visit. *'You will get your next instructions when I see you. BA.'*

He had visited one of his old buddies in the prison before and was careful of what he took with him. After going through security, he made his way to the visitor's area and waited for Brian to enter.

Brian sat down opposite him. "Thanks for coming. Have you checked in on Henrietta and the kids?"

"Yes, I have."

Speaking quietly Brian said, "Every Tuesday Henry and Benjamin leave the premises at 9am and drive to Benjamin's mothers' monument. They are away from the property for approximately 30 minutes. The security detail also goes with them."

"I need you to pay particular attention to what I am about to tell you. There is an entrance on the western side fence where there are no cameras. The house is two hundred metres from the gate. You need to drive your vehicle up to the veranda and leave it there."

With a look of intrigue on his face Robert asked, "how do you know this?"

Without raising his voice, but somehow still managing to show his annoyance, Brian replied, "because I used to sneak in to see Susan. I never got into her room but could hear her talking to herself inside. Even if I saw her, she only knew me as Agent Allan and not her father. Now, if I can continue!"

Brian took a moment to compose himself before he went on. "I'm hoping that Henry hasn't changed the house security code. This is important. Remember these numbers: eight … seven … two … nine. When you get home write the numbers down, turn the paper around and write what you see backwards, exactly as you see it."

Wiping his brow, he then instructed, "when you walk under the long veranda, you will see the security panel on the right side close to the door. Once inside, Susan's room is the first on the left, you can't miss it. Whenever they leave the premises, they give Susan a mild sedative. She is awake and should be calm. Offer her a bar of chocolate, that should keep her happy.

"Don't forget once you are inside you have 20 minutes before they return. Do you still have the key I gave you to the old warehouse property at Pyrmont?"

"Yes, it's in my desk draw at home" Robert replied.

Casually glancing at the clock on the wall, Brian realised there were only fifteen minutes remaining for this visit.

"No-one else is here, are you special or something?" Robert asked.

"Very funny, smart arse. I am not with the general prison population. Now shut the fuck up and pay attention. Inside the warehouse there are soundproof rooms upstairs including separate bathrooms. Before you get Susan, move your things into the warehouse. Her medication is already at the warehouse so make sure you read the instructions carefully!"

"I'll take my gear to the warehouse tomorrow and set everything up" Robert replied.

"Did you attend the auction?" Brian asked.

"Yes, but it was called off not long after everyone arrived. I introduced myself as Robert, but Benjamin didn't buy it."

"I take it then that Henry wasn't there. If Benjamin wasn't expecting you, he would have contacted Henry. Which is why Benjamin called the event off."

"Yeah. PK was there too. If it wasn't for him, I would have been wearing cement shoes and be at the bottom of the river," PK excitedly added.

"I'm counting on you, don't stuff this up! Text me when the job is done" Brian said as he stood to leave the room.

After leaving the prison, and arriving back at his car, he started writing notes on a pad. Remembering what Brian had said about the code, he wrote it down before turning the paper around and writing exactly what he saw backwards - PSr8.

CHAPTER

8

Detective Adams heard the cheering as he entered the large open plan office.

Standing at the door of his office door Area Commander Phillip Morgan called, "welcome back Martin".

Detective Spencer stepped forward and reached out to shake Martin's hand. "Joe Spencer, great to meet you".

"Ok, listen up. For those of you who don't know Detective Adams has returned from leave and will be assisting us with the Belltrees bunker fire incident," the area commander continued. Looking at Detective Adams, he said, "Martin, walk with me".

Opening the door to Interview Room 4, door he said, "I have set you up in here. Relative file notes, crime scene photos and anything else related to the case are in these boxes. Let me know if there is anything you need".

Detective Adams opened a box tagged 'Dr Marinov'. *Let's start at the beginning.* "Wow! Haven't seen one of these for a long time", he said to himself as he placed a cassette player on the table.

He found a power socket and plugged in the cassette player and placed cassette 1 into the device. He hit play and began listening. There was a loud humming sound that lasted only a few seconds, and then the recording began. The recording was a bit scratchy but still audible.

Opening one of Dr Marinov's journals the detective began reading events tracking the daily routine carried out on what was labelled Subject 1, female 20 years. Pages also included discussions with a man called Henry.

Completely overwhelmed by the narrator's written and verbal statement, he stared at the ceiling before compiling his own set of notes.

Scratching his head, he muttered to himself, "people think this only happens in the movies!"

After digging around for a while, he decided to put his notepad to one side and make use of the board for taking notes. Talking out loud, he wrote on the whiteboard:

Porta Augusta News 31 December 1993

20-year-old woman, Clare Hanson reported missing after failing to collect her 3-year-old son Benjamin from local day care centre in Porta Augusta. Her body was never found; Coroner's report declared her death 2001

After several attempts of tracing Benjamin Hanson through South Australian Child Protection Service records, the disgruntled detective decided to widen his search to include South Australian Adoption records.

After finally receiving confirmation from the protective service agency, he returned to the whiteboard to add that Benjamin Hanson had been adopted by Henry White in 1995.

Opening a box of case files, the detective came across a file titled *Benjamin White, bunker personnel – interview* and began reading Benjamin's statement.

Talking under his breath he said, *Mm Benjamin worked in the bunker with Dr Marinov!"*

Returning to the board he added:

Dr Marinov (Scientist) → Benjamin White (handler) → Gavin → Henry ? involvement.

Excitedly he left his office and knocked on Area Commander Phillip Morgan's office door.

"I have found a connection between Benjamin and Henry. When Benjamin was a 3-year-old boy his mother was reported missing. A Coroner's report declared her death in 2001. Coincidentally in the same year Benjamin Hanson was adopted by a Henry White."

Nodding in support the Commander replied, "good work Detective!"

CHAPTER

9

It's 7am Tuesday morning. Today is the day that Robert has one chance to kidnap Susan. There was no text on paper to read, just his mental notes that he nervously repeated over and over to himself.

Giving himself forty-five minutes to drive to the property, he arrived with ten minutes to spare. Waiting in bushland near the back gate, he watched his phone dancing to a theme song, Eye of the Tiger.

Accepting the call, he was surprised by the voice, "Robert it's PK. Brian thought you may need a little help today. I can see your car, I'm just off to your left. Flashing my headlights now."

Annoyed Robert muttered, "I don't need backup!"

Replying to PK, he said, "I prefer to work alone, but seeing as you are here, see you at the gate in two minutes!"

As he approached the gate, he noticed that PK was smoking a joint. "For fuck's sake. I hope you're not high PK?"

"Nah. It's cool mate. Don't worry about me," PK replied.

"Also, just so you know, I've been here before with Brian."

Retrieving an A4 sheet from his backpack, PK offered Robert a peek. After reading it, he was annoyed he didn't think of it himself as he tilted his head to the side and said, "ransom note. Clever!"

Watching Henry and his security detail drive away, PK opened the gate and hitched a ride up to the veranda.

"You know your way far better than me, so I'll leave you to do your thing and I'll get Susan. Meet back here in fifteen minutes," Robert said.

Nodding, PK left him at the veranda and began making his way to Henry's office.

Trashing people's places was nothing new for PK. As he had become homeless at a young age, he had mastered the art of breaking into houses, leaving them disorganised but not vandalised.

First things first. He said a clown mask from his pocket and slid it over his head before opening the door leading to Henry's office.

Dragging a chair across the floor and stopping just under the camera, he reached up and threw a black cloth over the camera and then began trashing the office. Once he was finished, he retrieved the ransom note from inside his jacket pocket, laid it on the desk, stabbing the paper with a pocketknife. Checking his phone, he saw he had five minutes to spare and stood at the door admiring his handiwork before exiting the room.

Meanwhile at the other end of the building Robert had cautiously opened Susan's door and entered. Susan was lightly sedated but as she sat up, he instantly saw that although she was still a young girl on the outside, her facial expressions were gone.

Not truly appreciating Susan's ability to communicate and take instructions, he thought speaking in a soft voice would be his best option. "Hi Susan, my name is Robert. Would you like to go for a drive?"

Susan was initially wobbly on her feet but managed to stand and look Robert straight in his eyes. Slowly tilting her head to the side, and with a childlike voice she asked, "are we going to see Dr Alex?"

Hoping not to make the biggest mistake of his life he replied, "maybe!"

Susan took a step forward. "Ok."

With a sigh of relief, Robert stepped into the room. Turning his head slightly, he calmly said, "come on then!"

Susan followed, collecting a backpack on her way, dragging it behind her.

As they began their walk to the van, Robert checked his watch. Time was running out. There was only five minutes left to get Susan seated in the van.

PK was already back at the van when he saw Robert and Susan walking towards him. PK looked at his watch he said, "you just made it dude."

Robert opened the sliding door and secured Susan inside the vehicle.

PK tapped Robert on the shoulder. "Ok, looks like both our jobs are done. I'm out of here now" he said before running back to the gate, hopping in his car, and driving away.

Robert turned the ignition. As he looked in the rear-view mirror he sighed to himself. *What are you?* He thought, before driving off the property and towards the highway.

CHAPTER

10

Henry was giving Benjamin a roasting about taking PK to the auction, again reminding him that he couldn't be trusted when Theo, his driver, stopped the vehicle and called out to him. "Sir, something is wrong. Stay in the vehicle."

Francesca, the cleaner frantically waved her arms as she ran towards to the vehicle.

"Francesca what is wrong?" Theo asked.

"When I arrive today … I park my car in usual spot. I saw a black van drive away." She pointed at the back gate excitedly, and said, "it drove out back gate."

"Ok, get in your car and lock the door. Wait there until I come and get you."

Returning to Henry and Benjamin, Theo said, "Francesca saw a van leaving the property. Stay here, I'm going to walk the perimeter and then enter the building."

"Benjamin, go with him," Henry ordered!

A short while later, after walking the perimeter, Theo touched his radio earpiece, and told Henry the perimeter was intact and showing no signs of entry to the outer buildings.

"Benjamin isn't back yet, so I don't have an update on inside the house," he continued.

This worried Henry. It worried him so much that he decided to phone one of his crooked buddies in the police force. Dialling his number, he was surprised when Dan answered the call straight away.

"Henry is everything ok?" Dan asked anxiously.

"I'm not sure. Someone has been on my property. My driver and Benjamin are checking it out now."

Still on the phone to Dan, Henry exited his car and loudly called out to Benjamin on his earpiece, ""talk to me Benjamin. Has anyone been inside the house?"

Benjamin replied, "yes, your office has been ransacked. I'm just heading out the back of the building to check on Susan."

There was a brief pause and then, "She's gone! Susan is gone!"

"Henry, you knew in the beginning that no matter how many security procedures you put in place, there was always going to be some risk" Dan said.

"Yes, I know," he responded. "Any chance you can drop by and watch the CCTV footage with Benjamin?"

Dan looking at his watch and said, "I can be there in forty-five minutes. In the meantime, check and see if there is anything missing from your office."

CHAPTER

11

Henry had finished talking with Dan and was heading towards the building when Benjamin called out on the radio, "Henry you need to come to your office now!"

Upon entering the office Henry said, "hell, it's a bloody mess!"

"It wasn't just a break-in. Whoever it was also left a ransom note for you." Benjamin passed a note to him.

Reading the note out loud Henry said, "$500,000.00 and you get Susan back. There is no negotiating. Further instructions to follow."

"This was a well-planned break-in. They disarmed the alarm at 9:05 am. There must have been two intruders. I think they both entered via the veranda end of the building. One stayed at that end getting Susan, while the other walked through the house, entering and trashing the office, leaving the ransom note. They knew the exact day and exact time that we would be away from the property. Francesca arrived here at 9:30 am and saw the vehicle leave" Benjamin said.

Using the intercom, Theo announced that he had sent Francesca home and that Dan had arrived, and he was on his way to the office.

Henry, Dan and Benjamin all stood in the observation control room as Theo brought up the CCTV footage. "Sir, this is the footage from today. I have fast forwarded to 8:55 am, the time we left this morning."

Scrolling forward Theo stopped at 9:10 am. "Here you see a masked intruder opening the office door. After entering, you can see they didn't look around the room checking for a camera. I would say this person has been here before. Also, this is where it gets interesting. Look closely, as the person reaches up to throw a black cloth over the camera, there is a simple stick figure tattoo on the inner part of his right forearm."

Benjamin stood and covered his face with his hands. "PK, that's fucking PK!"

Slapping the back of Benjamin's head, Henry yelled "PK! First you took him to the auction which I strongly disagreed with and now this. Have I not taught you anything son?" Henry turned his back on Benjamin. "Get out of my sight!"

CHAPTER

12

It was nearly midday when Robert approached the Pyrmont warehouse complex via the rear driveway. Behind the tinted windows of the van, he checked the rear-view mirror and was pleased to see that Susan had not stirred during the entire journey.

Ahead, there appeared to be a traffic jam that was preventing him from entering the warehouse complex parking lot. "What the fuck," he muttered angrily, manoeuvring the van past the endless line of cars waiting to access McDonalds drive thru.

Finally, off the road, he used the remote to open the large warehouse door and parked the van in a corner out of the way. The hardest part was about to begin, getting Susan out of the van without incident.

Sliding the van door open he was surprised to see that she appeared relatively calm. There was something beyond that face that intrigued him, and he was interested in learning more about her. There was still a sense of vulnerability and innocence about this young girl.

Robert knew she was used to wearing a leash, and he'd remembered to bring one with him. Using a softly spoken voice he secured the leash to her collar and asked if she would like to get out of the van. She shrugged her shoulders and hopped out, viewing her surroundings without uttering a word.

Susan shivered. It wasn't cold, it was just her imagination. She hadn't been out of her room that separated her from the outside world for a while.

Feeling comfortable but still wary of her, he wanted to reassure Susan that she was safe.

Leading her to her room, he opened the door and invited her in. She entered before turning to face him and said, "I have been here before. Is it lunch time?"

"You go sit at your table and I will bring something in shortly," he replied, abruptly leaving the room.

Robert shot a disapproving look as PK walked into the warehouse.

"Like what you've done with the place," PK sarcastically unannounced.

"What are you doing here PK?"

"Yeah, well Allan asked me to drop by once Susan was here. I see she has settled into her new home ok."

"Where are you going?" Robert asked loudly as PK started walking across the floor towards Susan.

Susan's eyes lit up when she saw PK. "PK! Did you bring Dr Alex with you?" she asked.

PK turned back towards Robert in frustration. "She doesn't know?"

"Give me a break, I've only just met the girl."

PK joined her in the room.

Robert asked, "do you think that's wise?"

"We have a good relationship. I'm her friend and I want it to stay that way."

Susan leapt up, hugging PK closing the door behind him and saying, "that's better. Have you got any lollies?" she innocently asked.

He lifted a bag of hot chips and extended it towards her. "Here, eat up before they get cold. I'm sure you're hungry."

Robert began walking away when his mobile rang.

"Hi Robert, Susan settled in, and ok? Brian asked.

"Would've been nice if you told me PK was going to pop in."

"He's Susan's friend. It's important that she feels safe."

"OK, now go into the small office near the door. There is some paperwork you need to be familiar with in case of an intrusion."

Entering the office, Robert sighed as he located the paperwork on the filing cabinet.

"Light reading, not!" he muttered under his breath.

"I heard that. Stop whinging!" Brian said and then disconnected the call.

CHAPTER

13

Matt and Doug, two local golfers were heading up a side road near Wakehurst golf course when a teenage girl ran from the bushes screaming for someone to phone the police.

Golf club flailing and hitting the ground in the hope of maintaining his balance Matt approached the teenager. "Take a breath, tell me what's wrong?"

"There's a lady in the bushes. Call the police," she repeated over and over.

Doug pointed to the bushy area on the left and asked, "in here"?

"Yes!" she replied, sobbing.

"Matt, call 000," Doug requested as he crouched down and walked into the bushy terrain.

On the far side there was a small clearing the size of a cubby house where he could see a woman with her chin resting on her upper chest.

All three waited on the road, Doug waving as the police car neared.

"I'm Constable Andrews and this is my partner Constable Toms," the nearest officer announced, gesturing to his female partner. "You called 000 sir?"

"Yes Constable. The young girl here ran from the scrub. She was very distressed and saying she saw a lady in the bushes," Matt said.

Doug pointed in the direction of the body. "On the other side of these trees there is a clearing on the right where I saw a woman sitting upright with her back against a tree. She appears to have a head wound."

Before Constable Andrews made his way through the thick scrub, he suggested he remained with his friend back at the side road where he would shortly join them.

Putting gloves on to ensure he did not to disturb the area, the constable approached the woman and established that she was deceased. He secured the crime scene using police tape and began collecting samples and enclosing them in evidence bags.

Talking into his two-way radio, the constable advised the radio room of his location, confirming that the deceased woman approximately twenty-five to thirty years old found and requested detectives to attend.

The constable then returned to the side road. "Let us talk with the young girl first and then I will take your statements."

The female police officer walked over to the girl. "My name is Constable Toms. What's your name?"

The young girl was shaking as she replied, "my name is Julie, Julie Wilkins."

Placing a hand on the girls shoulder, Constable Toms continued, "Julie let's walk over to the police car. There you go. Please have a seat." Can you tell me what happened?"

"I was taking a short cut through the bushes on my way to my friend's place when I saw her."

"You're doing really well. Julie, do you live at home with your parents?"

"I live with my mum."

"Why don't we give her a call, ask her to come and take you home?"

Julie took her phone from her pocket and tapped on contacts. The constable said, "how about I speak with your mum?"

The constable told Julie's mother that they would take Julie to the police station and requested she join her, at which time Julie could make a formal statement.

After taking statements from Doug and Matt both were allowed to leave the area but were reminded that the detectives may want to follow up with them shortly.

The lead Detective Samantha Taylor arrived at the crime scene and headed over to speak with the constables. "What can you tell me?"

"Two spent shell cases fired from a small calibre gun. One bullet wound to the head; the other bullet is lodged in the tree behind the body. Smashed mobile phone laying in the grass, hopefully we can get something from the prints on the glass. Small bag of what looks like weed found beside the body. No ID, we will check in the items that we have collected. Hopefully DNA will help us."

Taking gloves from her pocket Detective Taylor leaned over the body. "Oh, what do we have here?" She removed a white card and placed it in an evidence bag.

"Interesting, one side of the card is blank, on the flipside numbers appear. Too long for a mobile number or bank account number."

"Who found the body?" the detective asked.

Opening his notepad the constable replied, "young girl taking a short cut through the bush. Her name is Julie Wilkins. Julie is currently at the police station waiting for her mother to arrive at which time she will make a statement."

Calling out the other constable said, "Detective, there are fresh tyre tracks over here."

Detective Taylor nodded and phoned Forensics requesting their presence at the crime scene. "Forensics are on their way. We need a cast of those tyre tracks. Let's hope they can identify the type of vehicle used. Can you also ask the manager of the golf club for access to CCTV camera footage?"

Looking at Detective Taylor, the constable said, "Will do. We have collected samples and will also give these to Forensics for testing."

"Thanks. Forensics will hopefully fill in the blanks. Please leave a copy of your report on my desk." Detective Taylor replied, walking away from the scene.

CHAPTER

14

Benjamin stood in his study. He was trying to build up the courage to phone Henry and tell him that not only was Susan still missing but also, PK has not been sighted at any of his usual haunts.

Taking a deep breath, he dialled henry's mobile number, hoping he wouldn't pick up. It rang once ... twice ... three times. He was about to hang up when he heard Henry's voice. "I gather you have good news for me" he said.

"Hi Pops."

"I've told you not to call me that!" Henry interrupted. "Have you found out who took Susan or not?"

"No. Word was that there may be something going down at Pyrmont. I sent Stephen and David to the location. I'm waiting for Stephen to get back to me with an update."

"Get Susan back! I don't care how you do it!" he yelled before ending the call and slamming the phone down.

Benjamin was used to changing his appearance. Opening a draw, he pulled out a wallet and disguise. He looked at the photo ID inside. "Today I'm Richard Morris," he said to himself as he changed his persona and headed to his local police station.

Standing at the entrance to Belrose Police Station a police constable opened the door and welcomed him in.

"Thank you," he said in an English accent. He entered and stood at the reception desk.

The duty constable greeted him saying, "hello sir how may I help you?"

Continuing his persona he said, "I am here to report that my friend has gone. Mm mm, I haven't seen him for a few days, and I am worried about him."

Fumbling with his wallet it fell open, revealing his fake ID.

"Mr Morris, let's get some details about you and your friend. What's your friends full name and address?" she asked.

"His name is Perry King."

"Where does Mr King live?"

"I am not sure."

"Does he have any family that we may be able get to contact with?"

Becoming agitated and letting his English accent slip, Mr Morris, AKA Benjamin White barked at the constable, "look forget it. I will try and find him myself."

Once he had left the Police Station, the duty constable brought her concerns to the attention of the desk sergeant.

"Let's check the national database," he said.

Searching the name, Perry King they were both surprised to see the name appear a few times. One listing that caught the desk sergeant's attention was Perry King AKA PK.

CHAPTER

15

Stephen and David were quietly hiding behind a full loaded skip on a deserted building site at Pyrmont. Feeling like he was going to puke David looked at Stephen and said, "mate, the skip stinks. This stench is horrific!"

Stephen was ignoring David and looking at a text that had popped up on his mobile screen. "Right on time! Black SUV two minutes away heading in our direction."

"I have been working with you now for a few months, but I still don't know what the shipment is."

"After the bunker fire at Belltrees, Henry and Benjamin decided to keep both Gavin and Susan. Henry had a break-in. Benjamin *did* entertain some of his friends at his place. Perhaps he did drop a few lines and disclose Henry's set up. After entering his property, they trashed the place and took Susan with them. This was an organised break-in as they knew exactly where she was located. A ransom note was found in Henry's office along with instructions that they had twenty-four hours to transfer the money in exchange for her. They've also sent a short video confirming they have her! Henry transferred the money this morning. Our job now is to collect her!"

David saw a vehicle approaching. Something was telling him this was a set-up. Sensing that Stephen was about to make the biggest mistake of his life he said, "something isn't right here mate!

Something just moved. Far left-hand side of the parking area near the stairs. Looks like a watch glistening in the sun. Look, there it is again! Did you tell your contact that we would be hiding behind this skip? If you didn't then perhaps the guy across the road is here to collect and you have both been duped."

A figure emerged from near the stairs across the road and began staggering to the roads edge.

"Look, he's just a harmless drunk!" Stephen said, pointing at the man.

"How many drunks do you see carrying a weapon in their hand" David asked cautiously.

"Hey, here comes the black SUV."

Before he could make a move, David tugged at Stephen's shirt and said, "wait!"

"That looks like one of Eddie's boys behind the wheel." Stephen hissed angrily.

"Hey, look there is someone sitting in the cargo tray of the SUV. It's a woman and … shit she's armed. With a semi-automatic."

A male voice could be heard yelling from inside the SUV. "Fire! Fire!"

The woman made no attempt to shoot, just sat lifeless in the back of the cargo tray.

Suddenly the passenger door of the SUV opened. The man was gunned down and the vehicle sped off down the lane.

Stephen was overwhelmed with emotion and decided to phone Benjamin. Dialling his number, he found there was no answer. "Come on, pick up! Going voice mail!"

"Benjamin, this was a set-up. An SUV arrived at the pick-up point, with one of Eddie's boys behind the wheel. There was a woman was sitting in the back cargo area armed with a semi-automatic but made no attempt to shoot. Phone me back. Now."

After what seemed like an eternity, Benjamin's name popped up on his phone. "About time!"

"Calm down and tell me exactly what happened," Benjamin replied.

"David and I waited at the deserted building site at Pyrmont as you instructed, but there was someone else at this location. He looked like a drunk, but as David pointed out, how many drunks carry guns?"

"An SUV drove past him in the laneway. It looked like they were going to use this woman to eliminate anyone present at the pick-up point, but that failed as she didn't respond to the command to fire. A passenger in the SUV then gunned down the man. Looks like more than one party were here to collect and both have been double-crossed. "Do you want David and I to pay Eddie a visit?"

"Fuck!" Benjamin yelled. Do whatever it takes to get Susan back."

CHAPTER

16

Commander Phillip Morgan was sitting at his desk when his mobile phone vibrated in his jacket pocket. Only one person would be contacting him now, his undercover officer. "This must be very important for you to call me."

"Yes sir. We need to meet."

"Tonight 10pm. Corner of Cook Road and Centennial Lane," the commander barked and abruptly ended the call.

David was familiar with the area and arrived a little before the meeting time, giving him time to reminisce about his last visit. It had been as a teenager, watching the woodchopping competition.

The commander up behind David and flashed his headlights.

David hopped into the back seat of the vehicle.

"Your call sounded urgent," the Commander said.

"What can you tell me about what happened after the bunker fire and in particular the two candidates, Gavin and Susan?"

"After the fire, the surviving scientists and participants including Gavin and Susan were relocated to a safe house. Brian Allan, an ASIO agent who was working with a father and son team - Henry and Benjamin White - removed them and took them to another location. The agent wasn't aware that a tracking device had been placed under the vehicle. Intelligence advised that Allan had gone rogue and was working with one of the handlers, who we later discovered was also working with the mastermind of the experiment. Why do you ask?"

"An intruder broke into Henry White's place and trashed the joint. They kidnapped Susan. A ransom note was left stating he had twenty-four hours to transfer money in exchange for her. To me this sounds personal. I think the intruder and Henry may know each other."

"Earlier today, Stephen got a tip-off about collecting Susan. Stephen and I waited at the location. Someone else was waiting in the laneway. It smelled like a set-up. A black SUV drove down the laneway but a woman - not Susan - was sitting in the back and armed with a semi-automatic. A passenger from the vehicle then opened the door and gunned down the man in the laneway. We didn't see the passenger's face, but we have a lead. The question is, is PK involved?"

"What correctional centre is Brian Allan being held? It would be interesting to see if Allan has had any visitors lately."

"What are you thinking?" the commander asked.

"Before the bunker fire, you said that Allan was working with Henry and Benjamin White. Allan would have frequently visited Henry's place and would have known the set-up as well as his business contacts. My question is, is there a disgruntled business partner that Allan may have kept in contact with? Maybe they visited Allan in prison? Together they could have orchestrated this "so-called" ransom note and set up the double-cross meeting at Pyrmont."

"Good point. I'll check on that and get back to you."

CHAPTER

17

Robert knew there were two subjects from the Belltrees bunker that had been transformed. Deciding it was time to peek inside Benjamin's house, he took up his position a few houses down the road.

Ensuring the coast was clear, Robert picked up his backup before exiting the van and approaching the house. He thought it was strange that there didn't appear to be any CCTV cameras at the front of the property.

He climbed over a side fence and slipped into the backyard. He kept looking at all aspects of the side of the house. One mistake could not only ruin his chances of looking inside the house, but he could be captured or even killed.

Once inside the house he noticed all the blinds were drawn and the house was divided into two sections. The first section appeared to be a normal structure. The second had an entirely different set-up. There were two rooms each separated by glass petitions. In front of each room was an out-of-place set of dilapidated set of drawers.

The first room was empty, but it was what was inside the second room that caught his attention. Seeing his reflection in the glass he said to himself, "well now, here is the most important room in the house!"

Running his hands down the glass, he was convinced that there were no hidden alarms attached.

He only took his eyes off the glass room for a few seconds when he realised who was inside.

Robert saw a man that he could only describe as 'the lights are on, but no-one is home.' "Wow, I knew about Susan, but I don't know anything about you," he muttered to himself, struggling to decide how he was going to remove the man from the house.

The man didn't say a word. He approached the glass door and waited.

"I'll take that as a yes," Robert replied.

Using the same technique as he had when he took Susan, he opened his backpack and removed some bottled water. He offered it to Gavin. Looking around the room he found a leash. He carefully placed it around Gavin's neck. "Ok, let's go."

Robert looked around as they approached the front of the house. Once he had ensured the coast was clear, he opened the door and led Gavin to the vehicle.

Once inside the van he noticed that Gavin appeared to become a little drowsy. To help him feel more at ease, he turned on the radio and tuned in an FM music station.

Some forty minutes later they arrived at the warehouse. Robert used the remote to open the large warehouse door and parked the van in the corner as he had when he'd arrived with Susan.

Seeing that Gavin was starting to rouse, Robert told him that Susan was looking forward to seeing him.

Gavin's demeanour did not change. Robert carefully removed Gavin from the van and walked Gavin to his new room and securing him inside.

Feeling pleased with himself, he got back in the van and decided to turn on the radio, singing to the tune currently playing.

CHAPTER

18

It was early evening when David and Stephen slowly drove past 73 Pringle Street. The garage door was closed. "Well, well, well, look at what is parked on the grass. A black SUV ute with an open cargo area," Steven said, turning their vehicle around and parking opposite. "Let's talk about how this is going to play out. Looks like no reinforcements are presently onsite, which means we need to get in and out quickly and hopefully quietly. No using our firearms unless there is no alternative."

Stephen walked around the side the side of the house and looked through the side window. 'What the!" he said, crouching down and monitoring for David to stop. He pointed to the front of the house. They both looked in dismay as PK walked out of the house carrying two black bags.

Stephen creeped up behind PK, cocked his gun and pressed it against the back of PK's head. "What the fuck are you doing PK?"

Caught by complete surprise, PK dropped the bags and raised his arms in the air. Slowly turning around, he said "I heard you and David talking about how Eddie doubled-crossed you. Thought I could get your shipment back for you."

"I've never spoken to David nor anyone else about such a matter. So what do I do with you now?

"Ok, ok! I heard on the grapevine that a big shipment was coming in. You know what Eddie's boys are like. They have always been disloyal to him. So, I called in a favour from a mate who may have said the shipment was stolen and where to collect it. He gave them the wrong address. Eddie and I just got back from collecting the shipment."

"So, who did your mate tell?" Stephen asked.

"Ok! It was Benjamin. He took Gavin along with him and they went to the wrong address."

"Now if I was to go inside the house what would I find?" Steven asked.

"Eddie threatened me and told me he was going to cut me out of the deal. I couldn't let him do that!"

"Let's get going. If PK's prints are found inside, perhaps we can help the cops and drop him off at a Police Station." Stephen said to David.

Steven picked up the bags and placing them on the back seat. Turning to David, Stephen said, "gag him and tie him up. Put him in the boot. Once we get back to the house, I'll decide what to do with him."

CHAPTER

19

"David, it's late, crash here tonight mate. Tomorrow we'll decide what to do with our double-crosser," Stephen said as he looked across at PK still tied and gagged in the back corner of the house.

David was totally surprised when he saw Stephen remove a rug before unlocking and raising a small trapdoor with stairs leading to the basement.

"Leave him gagged and throw him downstairs. We'll deal with him later" Steven said as they prepared to leave the house.

The next morning, watching TV by the pool David dialled 101 and listened to his voice messages. It was the last voice message that made David stand to attention.

"David, I'm scared. PK attached me. I passed out and when I woke found that we were parked in bushland. I heard him talking to you on the phone. I'm hiding in the scrub."

"Someone is coming." They were the last words David heard before the call ended abruptly.

Finding Stephen, David said, "we have to talk to PK. He didn't drop Nat at home yesterday like he told me".

David opened the trapdoor, walked down the stairs, removed PK's gag, and grabbed him by the scruff of his shirt, pulling him upstairs. "Ok scumbag, where is my Natalie?"

"I told you mate. I dropped her off at her house." PK replied.

Picking up his phone, David set the volume to maximum as he replayed the 101-voice message.

"Now let's go over this again. Where is Natalie?" David shouted, pulling the gag from PK's mouth.

Before PK could reply, the words BREAKING NEWS flashed across the TV screen. The news reporter began her coverage by saying, "we now go live to Wakehurst where the body of a woman approximately aged twenty-five to thirty years old with blonde hair is wearing blue jeans and a pink sweater. This appears to have been an execution-style murder with a single bullet wound to the head. Police have set up a crime scene perimeter. No ID was found on the victim, but various items have been collected and taken in as evidence."

Stephen pushed David aside. "You have been a *busy* boy PK. You steal from me and murder Natalie. You *scumbag.*

What else have you been up to?" He punched PK in the face repeatedly forcing him to the floor.

"You think I work for you only? You are small fry compared to the kingpins I work for," PK replied with a big, bloody grin on his face.

"Stephen, if you kill him, we're not going to get any answers," David interjected.

Opening the trapdoor, Stephen said, "gag him again and throw him back downstairs. We'll decide his fate later!"

After closing the trapdoor David said, "the black bags PK took from Eddie's place are full of cocaine. I thought the shipment was Susan!"

"Eddie didn't know anything about Susan, and neither did PK. Where Eddie got the drugs from is a mystery to me. In saying that, we can make some money on the side, so it's a win-win for both of us."

CHAPTER

20

"Police, Fire or Ambulance?" the radio operator asked.

"Police!" a distressed man yelled back at the operator.

"What suburb and state are you calling from?" the operator asked.

"Northbridge, NSW!"

The operator asked him to stay on the line.

"Northbridge Police" a male voice announced. When there was no response, he repeated himself a little louder, "Northbridge Police!"

"I arrived to pick up a taxi fare at 77 Pringle Street when I heard gunfire coming from a nearby house! One man ran out of the house carrying black bags. Then I saw two men get out of a car that was parked on the other side of the road. One man picked up the bags while the other man tied up the first man and put him in the boot. Then they drove away."

"I am Constable Fry, what is your name sir?"

"Lee Song" the caller replied.

"Thank you. Where are you now Mr Song?"

"I drove away, pulled up down the road and called 000."

"Ok sir, the Police are on their way and will want to talk to you. Stay where you are."

Within a few minutes, multiple police cars with sirens blazing pulled into the street. One car stopped next to the taxi while the remaining vehicles continued to the reported address.

The house was dark except for a flickering light in a small room at the front of the dwelling. With guns drawn, eight police officers cautiously approached. Looking through an open window the lead signalled to his fellow officers that there was one person laying on the floor. Using hand signals, the lead officer pointed for four of his men to go around the back while the remaining officers stayed at the front of the house.

Once all officers were in place, he used his two-way radio to give the order to enter the house.

Simultaneously both rear and front doors were forced open as all officers called out "Police! Don't move, don't move!"

Curiosity was mounting across the road. A few on-lookers watched in silence until officers approached and requested that they move a safe distance away.

As the police exited the house from the front, the lead officer contacted the radio room requesting detectives attend the crime scene.

Approaching the taxi, an officer called out to the driver and said, "I'm Constable Hopkins, are you Mr Song?"

"Yes Constable."

After getting Mr Song's details, the constable asked, "can you tell me what you saw?"

"I arrived to pick up a fare at 77 Pringle Street when I heard gunfire coming from a nearby house. A man dressed in a black tracksuit ran out of a house carrying black bags. A white four-wheel drive pulled up on the other side of the road and two men got out. One man picked up the bags while the other man pushed the guy up against the car and forced something into his mouth. He tied him up then pushed him into the boot. The four-wheel drive then drove away."

"Can you tell me anything that stood out about these men Mr Song?"

"It was getting dark, but I definitely know that the two men got out of a white four-wheel drive."

"You have been a great help Mr Song." Passing him a card the constable said, "please call the station if you remember anything else."

Walking up to the crime scene the constable saw that the detectives had arrived and were talking to other police officers.

Joining in the conversation, the officer updated the detective by saying their only witness had given a vague description of the men standing outside the house.

"What are the chances of two incidents in two days in the same street? House invasion at 37 Pringle Street, looks like a case of mistaken identity. I'm going to wait for the forensics report but in the meantime, can you leave a copy of your incident report on my desk?" Detective Taylor requested. "Also, please check to see if there are any CCTV cameras on Pringle Street, especially leading up to both numbers 37 and 73."

CHAPTER

21

"Good afternoon, I'm Fiona Forrester, coming to you live from News Central Radio 101. Welcome to Midday!

"Breaking news just in: There has been another incident in Pringle Street, Northbridge. A man's body has been found in a house at 73 Pringle Street and the body of a woman approximately aged between twenty-five to thirty years old has been found near Wakehurst Golf Course.

"Channel 9 reporter Lee Baker is on the line. Lee what are Police saying about these two incidents?"

"Fiona, Pringle Street, Northbridge is in the news again with the body found at the 73 Pringle Street address. Police have not identified the name of the man but do believe this is gang related. Police believe this property was the original target and not the address of the mistaken identity incident last week.

"Police have also announced that the body of a twenty-five to third-year old woman was found near the Wakehurst

Golf Course. Police tape has been placed around the crime scene where the woman's body was found. First reports are that the woman died of a gunshot wound to the head. Police have collected samples from the crime scene. The identity of the woman has not yet been made public. Police have said at it is too early to tell but do not believe this murder is connected to either incident at Pringle St, Northbridge."

"Thank you, Lee.

"Hasn't our weather been unusual lately? Experts say Australia is in La Niña and we will have been experiencing higher than average rainfall on the eastern parts of our beautiful country. Speaking of climate, my special guest joining us today is, Professor Frank Johnson.

"Welcome to Midday Professor Johnson. Growing up in Sydney, I don't remember the temperatures being hot as they are now. Can you explain more about that?"

"Good afternoon, Fiona. Thanks for having me. As many of your listeners would be aware, we are in the midst of a climate crisis. Over 13,000 of the world's climate scientists have unanimously declared an emergency. Ecosystems are at risk of collapse and the world's food security is at risk. No doubt, your listeners would agree any emergency requires immediate action.

"Recently there have been severe hurricanes in Florida, and Australia has just been through the most catastrophic bush fire season on record. There is growing evidence that these events are all linked to climate change. Failure to drastically and immediately cut greenhouse gas emissions will make the current number of extreme weather events such as storms, wildfires, and ice melt routine occurrences. If we carry on with a business-as-usual scenario, many parts of our planet will soon become uninhabitable."

"I understand after you leave the studio you will be making your way to the airport. There are a couple of listeners on hold who have questions for you. Ronald you are on the air. You have a question?"

"Yes. Professor Johnson, what's the difference between climate change and global warming?"

"Hi, Ronald, that's an excellent question; one that I have been asked on many occasions. 'Global warming' refers to the rise in global temperatures due mainly to the increasing concentrations of greenhouse gases in the atmosphere. 'Climate change' refers to the increasing changes in the measures of climate over a long period of time. For example, we measure the changes in precipitation, temperature, and wind patterns. I hope that answers your question, David."

"Belinda, you have a question?!

Hi Professor Johnson, do scientists all agree on climate change?"

"Hi Belinda, That's another excellent question. Ninety-nine percent of currently publishing climate scientists agree that human activities - the burning of fossil fuels - is responsible for current rapid warming. This reinforces the results of earlier surveys conducted by Dr John Cook and Professor Naomi Oreskes."

"I've just got the nod from my secretary, unfortunately Professor Johnson needs to leave now. On your return to Australia, if you could squeeze time in, I'd love to have you back in the studio, Professor."

I'll ask my Secretary, Penny to contact you regarding me returning to your program."

"The lines are open listeners, give me a call now on 131101."

CHAPTER

22

Benjamin's suspicions were correct, an outsider was playing games with Henry. Arriving home after visiting an old rival he discovered an intruder had been in his house. Angry, he phoned Henry. "Gavin is gone!"

"After the bungled house invasion, I told you that you should have brought him here." Henry pulled on the buttons of his shirt. "Who knew that you were keeping him at your place?"

"The only people that have been at my place over the last few weeks are, Stephen, David and PK."

"I need you to be honest with me, do you think that Stephen, David or PK could have told anyone else that Gavin was at your place?"

"PK invited his friend Natalie over a couple of weeks ago. When I saw she was in my house I told PK to get rid of her. She won't talk though."

"How can you be so sure?" Henry asked.

"She's dead!" he replied.

"And what do you know about this David?"

"Steven has used him for a few jobs, says he is trust-worthy."

"You do some digging around. We've already lost Susan. We need to find Gavin and find him right now," Henry yelled.

"What if the same people that took Susan are behind this?"

"Look, I know you're upset about Susan, but you need to stay focused."

"We need help with this. I'll contact Dan and get him to check your CCTV footage."

After hanging up Henry immediately phoned Dan he announced, "We have been compromised; our security has been breached."

"I'm on my way!" Dan replied.

CHAPTER

23

"Mate, you've been on the outside up until now, but I think it's time you were part of the business," Stephen announced to David. Interested?"

"Absolutely!" David replied, a smile on his face.

"Go home and I'll be in touch soon." Stephen shook David's hand and then walked him to the front door.

Scribbling a few notes on a notepad, Stephen decided he would phone Benjamin to discuss offering David a spot in the business. He dialled the mobile number and in his best professional voice asked, "Can we meet up today?"

"I've told you never to call me on this number! 2pm at our usual meeting place, and Stephen come alone.

Stephen arrived early at the meeting point at Dawes Point Park. Mesmerised, as he watched people climbing the bridge, and was startled when Benjamin tapped on the window of his SUV. Instinctively, Stephen's right hand hugged the butt of his gun.

"What's so important that it couldn't wait until our weekly meeting on Friday?" Benjamin asked.

"I've been using David with some of the smaller jobs, and he has been quite useful. I received your message to check out 73 Pringle Street. We found KP at Eddie's place, looks like he did the dirty on Eddie and was going to take the shipment for himself. David helped secure him in my basement."

"What do you know about David?"

"I know he has been inside. Small time stuff. A mate of mine suggested I look him up and give him some work. I followed him one day walking down George Street where he came across two thugs trying to rob a convenience store. What convinced me to use him was his quick thinking, he covered his face before marching into the store and beat the crap out of the thugs. He crouched down and without the shop attendant realising, he stuffed some of the money in his pocket before handing the rest to the worker and leaving the store. He was cool and didn't create any suspicion."

"Ok, I'll give him a try. Bring him to the house tomorrow. I have a job he can do. If he stuffs it up, he is gone. Understand?"

David had just arrived home when a text message popped up on his phone. *You're in. I'll pick you up 10am tomorrow morning.*

Retrieving a SIM card from the glovebox David inserted it into a burner phone. Finding his contact, he phoned the number and left a voice message, "I'm in. 10am tomorrow morning. Be ready to follow. Body found in bushes, check the system for a Natalie Webb. Also, check for Perry King, known on the streets as PK." Ending the call David removed the SIM before discarding the phone in an otto bin.

CHAPTER

24

Entering the meeting room, Area Commander Phillip Morgan welcomed everyone before he started the morning briefing. "Detective Adams has been going over the files and notes connected to the Belltrees Incident. Martin, you're up."

Pointing at the board, Martin updated the room with the following:

"Missing person – Porta Augusta. On 31 December 1993.

Twenty-year old woman, Clare Hanson failed to collect her three-year old son Benjamin from a local day care centre. Her body was never found. The coroner's report declared her death in 2001.

South Australian Adoption records have confirmed Benjamin Hanson was adopted by a Henry White in 1995.

Interview with Benjamin White, bunker personnel – interview and began reading his statement (DNA on file).

Dr Marinov, Scientist (deceased) → Benjamin White (handler) -Gavin (DNA on file) - ? Henry White.

Dr Marinov's journals recorded 4 January 1994, twenty-year-old woman subject tortured. No further records identifying who this woman was. Subject – Benjamin Hanson's mother??"

"Now to current events, Martin can you also update the room on the mistaken identity incident?" the Commander asked.

"Two masked men forced their way into the home where they physically restrained the couple, mouths gagged, and hands tied behind their backs. During the assault one intruder did all the talking and even announced that his mate was mute. A point of interest is that he named his mate 'Gav'. Gav apparently grunted only and tilted his head from side to side. The leader's demeanour changed after a phone call when he was told he had the wrong street number. The assaulted couple are in hospital, both in a stable condition."

"Detective Walker can you attend the hospital for follow-up? Also check to see if we have had any luck with CCTV cameras on both sides of Pringle Street, especially leading up to both 37 and 73." And now on to the body found near Wakehurst golf course. Detective Taylor attended the scene, can you update the room please?"

Facing her colleagues, the detective opened her notebook and began reading from the top, "body of a deceased female approximately twenty-five to thirty years was old found in bushes near Wakehurst golf course.

Two spent shell cases were fired from a small calibre gun. One bullet wound to the head; the other bullet is lodged in the tree behind the body.

A smashed mobile phone found in the grass was also bagged as evidence, and a small bag of what looks like weed was found beside the body. It was also bagged for evidence. While there was no ID, white card was found in the deceased's sleeve. One side is blank, but there are numbers on the flipside. This was bagged for evidence. Tyre tracks were found near the body. Samples were sent to the lab, and we will hopefully identify the type of vehicle used. I'll follow up with the golf course to see if their CCTV monitors the side road."

"There have been reports of gunfire at 73 Pringle Street, Northbridge. The eyewitness reported a man dressed in a dark tracksuit running out of the house carrying black bags. Two men exited a white four-wheel drive. One man picked up the bags. The other man pushed him up against the car, tying and gagged him before pushing him into boot of car." What are the chances of two incidents in same street in as many days? First, the mistaken identity at 37 Pringle Street and then gunfire at 73 Pringle Street. Payback perhaps? I have asked forensics for an update ASAP! I'll also follow up with CCTV footage on Pringle Street."

Clearing his throat, the commander stood up and said, "I can share with you that we have one of our own working undercover. To protect him and his cover I can't tell you much more other than to say he has gained the trust of a crime organisation boss. I am his only contact and the intel he just sent me indicates there is a link between the mistaken identity incident, the dead woman in the bushes at the golf course and the body found at 73 Pringle Street. Before you head out, leave your case files with Detective Adams. He will follow up your CCTV enquiries. Stay safe everyone!"

CHAPTER

25

Heavy traffic forced Stephen to phone David from his car to alert him he was running late. Going to voice male he said, "David, it's Stephen. It's 10am. I'm on my way but there is a pile up of traffic. May get to your place a bit late. Our meeting with Benjamin is scheduled for 11am. See you soon."

David was sitting on his front porch when Stephen arrived at his house. Nodding his head, David approached the car when Stephen hopped out and said, "sorry mate but you're going to have to wear a hood for the car ride to the house."

Stephen put the hood on David's head, tying the hood at the back before opening the black limo door and assisting him into the car.

David was trying to keep track of the direction the car was taking him. He felt the car had headed in an easterly direction for about twenty minutes before making what felt like a wide left-hand turn in a westerly direction. Traffic noise and suburban traffic began to peter out.

Towards the end of the journey all he could hear was the sound of screeching galahs.

After entering a large underground parking area, Stephen announced, "we have arrived, you can remove your hood now."

Even though the parking area was not well lit, it took David a few minutes for his eyes to adjust to the sudden light. He counted a security detail of six as a large swarthy appearing guard with a three-dot tattoo on his neck appeared and made an announcement on a two-way radio that the pair had arrived. Before proceeding inside both men were instructed to walked through a full-body scanning device where they also had to relinquish their mobile phones.

Once inside they were met with yet another security detail. After being ushered into a small meeting room that looked very much like an interrogation room, David realised this was a highly organised criminal organisation.

Stephen's annoyance of how he was treated seemed to indicate that he now understood that he was most likely ranked at the bottom of the organisation.

A thick set man entered the room and stood behind Benjamin. Stephen was clearly uncomfortable. Sitting opposite them, Benjamin placed a gun on the table. A nagging feeling came over David. This was not going to be a meet and greet engagement.

"Who have you told about Henry's organisation?" Benjamin asked.

"The only people I confided in are David and PK. Benjamin, I would never betray you or Henry," Stephen replied.

"I think that's bullshit!"

Ignoring Stephen, Benjamin turned his head to face David. Without warning, and without breaking eye contact with David, Benjamin picked up his gun. Before David could react, Benjamin had shot Stephen execution style.

"This is what happens when you get sloppy" Benjamin bent down to remove keys and a burner phone from Stephen's pockets. When he was done, he beckoned for the security detail to remove the body.

Handing the keys and phone to David he said, "this is your only method of communication. Your first job is to get rid of PK. Message me from this burner phone when the job is done. Ralph will drive you back to the city."

Placing the hood on David's head again, Ralph proceeded to drive him back to the city.

There was no sound during the journey. The only time he spoke was when they arrived at Central Railway Station. Before unlocking the door, he pulled the hood from his head and ordered, "get out!"

CHAPTER

26

David was out walking a friend's dog when an incoming call popped up on the burner phone screen.

"Where are you? I have a job for you!" Benjamin said.

Not wanting to a lie, he explained, "I'm walking a friend's dog! Wait, are you at my place?"

"Yes! Get back here now!"

"On my way." He and Sacha – the pooch - hopped into his hotted up red Ford F-150 truck.

As David drove into his driveway, Benjamin exited his car with a grin on his face and said, "didn't kind of think you would be a F-150 truck kind of guy!"

After letting Sacha into the backyard and walking towards his front door David asked, "you want a beer?"

Inviting Benjamin in, David ensured his police undercover work laptop and phone were not visible and were securely stashed under the floorboards in the living room.

"Make yourself at home. I'll get you that beer," he said as both men entered the modest living area of the house.

Not amused by his *so-called hotshot cocky attitude*, Benjamin waved away the offer of a beer and dropped an open file onto the coffee table. "I believe this guy, Robert Burns has something that belongs to me. Everything you need to know about him is in this file. Don't forget to check out the old warehouse at the Pyrmont address."

"I want to know everything about him. Where he goes, who he meets, and most importantly if he takes anything or anyone with him. Text me photos of everyone he meets. Do you understand?"

"Yes. One question though, there is no photo ID. How do I know I am following the right person? You said he had something that belonged to you. Who or what am I looking for?"

"You'll know if you see it. Oh, and another thing, you have forty-eight hours. Understand?" he barked abruptly and left the house.

Once he heard Benjamin's car leave the driveway, David retrieved his laptop and logged into the national database to run a quick search on Robert Burns using the date of birth Benjamin had supplied.

So astounded by what he saw, he sat back in his chair, cleared his throat and shook his head in amazement.

Then he dialled the commander's mobile. "C'mon! c'mon pick up."

When the commander picked up the call, David spoke without waiting for the commander to speak, "we have to meet now!"

CHAPTER

27

After managing to label both burner phones, David admired his handiwork. He sipped his latte and waited for his contact to arrive.

As he reviewed the notes on his phone, he saw the unmarked police car turn into the coffee shop carpark. As the commander left his car, David observed the tall man with greyish hair and decided that he did look in good shape for his age.

Waving inconspicuously as to not attract attention, the commander eventually sat, and David began sharing his notes.

"Went to what I believe may be the organisation headquarters yesterday. Unfortunately, I was travelling blind; as I had a hood over my head. I felt the car was possibly heading in an easterly direction for twenty minutes or so, and then possibly heading in a westerly direction. Traffic noise became less; possibly heading out of the suburbs."

"I counted a security detail of six when we exited the carpark. One guard had a three-dot tattoo on his neck. We had to walk through a full-body scanning device, and we had to hand in our mobile phones. Once inside we met more of the security detail before being put in what looked like an interrogation room. He introduced himself as Benjamin. He gave me a demonstration of what they do to sloppy people. He shot Stephen dead in front of me."

"He gave me a burner phone and told me it was my only method of communication. My orders are to get rid of PK. My instructions are to message him when the job is done. A driver brought me back to the city and dropped me at Central Railway Station. Oh, I also have my first job."

David retrieved a file from his backpack and placed it on the table. As you can see there is no photo ID, only a name and date of birth. I asked who or what am I looking for. He said, *'you'll know if you see* it'."

"I have the address of an old warehouse at Pyrmont that I need to check out. He wants to know everything about him. Where he goes, who he meets, and most importantly if he takes anything or anyone with him. I have 48 hours."

The commander took a deep breath and exhaled slowly, playing with his empty coffee mug. "You're a cop first. Have you thought about how this is going to pan out?"

David pushed a sheet of paper across the table. "PK and I will be at this address. Have an unmarked car arrive at 10 am tomorrow. Throw PK and I in the back of the car. Make it look like it was one of Eddie's friends out for revenge. Pick a place where your guys can pull over, pull me out of the car and pretend to shoot me. You can pick me up later."

The commander stood up to leave. "Ok, message me if anything changes."

CHAPTER

28

When detectives arrived at Natalie Webb's address in Liverpool they were surprised to see the front door ajar. The detectives cautiously approached the doorway, guns drawn.

"Police! Is there anyone in the house?" Detective Taylor called out.

Entering, she again called out but there was no reply. As the detectives walked through the house, there were calls of "clear" as they checked all rooms. When they were satisfied that the house was empty, they began their check.

The house was quite sparse, with minimal furniture in each room. In the corner of the loungeroom, sitting precariously on a small coffee table, a pile of old TV Week magazines were covered in dust particles.

"Look at the dining table. A partially eaten sandwich and a half full coffee mug. She left without cleaning up. Did Natalie have an unexpected visitor?" Detective Taylor asked.

An old laptop lying under the lounge caught her attention. Placing it in an evidence bag she commented, "let's take this in as evidence. Hopefully digital forensics can help us learn a bit more about Natalie."

Two hairbrushes each with different colour hair were also bagged to be taken in for DNA analysis.

Hearing a female voice, the detectives stood still and waited for the woman to come into view.

An older lady with a look of complete surprise, stood in front of the detectives. "Police. I'm Detective Taylor and this is Detective Peters. You are?"

"Sylvia Webb, I live here with my daughter Natalie." Sylvia removed her ID from her handbag. Handing it to Detective Taylor she asked, "why are you here, is Natalie ok?"

"Please take a seat. When was the last time you saw your daughter?" she asked.

"Yesterday morning, I visited my son Cody in the city, and stayed with him and his wife last night."

"I'm afraid I have some bad news. Natalie was found dead yesterday."

Sylvia was shaking as she asked what happened to Natalie.

"I'm sorry I can't tell you anything more at the present time. Do you know if Natalie was meeting anyone yesterday?"

"Not that I am aware of. My daughter was troubled, got in with the wrong people a while back. I moved in with her a few months ago."

"Is there someone you can phone?" the detective asked.

Picking up her mobile she said, "I'll call Cody. Cody didn't like me living here. Natalie would sometimes have men visiting her. They would arrive and be either be drunk or high on drugs."

"We have Natalie's mobile phone. It's password protected; would you know the password by any chance?"

Stumbling through her words, and crying, Sylvia said "Natalie loves … mmm loved dogs … when she was a child we had a dog named Spud."

Detective Taylor handed Sylvia her card. "Thank you. Sylvia we are sorry for your loss. Call me if you think of anything that may help us with our investigation,"

CHAPTER

29

Detective Adams was reviewing the report notes for the mistaken identity incident when an excited tech approached his desk.

"Hi I'm Russell. We've have managed to get CCTV camera footage for both incidents in Pringle Street, Northbridge."

Detective Adams motioned towards the tech's desk. "Show me."

"Pull up a chair. First, this is the footage from 35 Pringle Street," Russell said as they sat side by side ready to begin watching the camera footage.

It was about thirty seconds into the footage when a dark coloured van pulled up outside 35 Pringle Street. Pressing the freeze button; Russell zoomed into the frame. Only the first two letters of the registration number plate were visible. Two men were clearly seen standing on the roadside of the van. One wearing a mask while the other struggled to secure his mask, allowing sufficient time to show the man's face.

Pressing play again they continued watching the footage. Both of the masked men entered number 37.

Fast forwarding to around thirty minutes, both of the men exited the house. Freezing and zooming in again, both men were clearly seen on the image.

"Now the footage for 73 Pringle Street, Northbridge isn't as clear as the first, and again I will show it to you in two parts" Russell said.

The footage showed a grey SUV with a dent on the driver's side front panel of the vehicle. Again, the registration number plate was obscured.

However, when Russell zoomed in, Detective Adams was surprised to see that the male sitting in the driver's seat had made no attempt to hide his face.

Russell zoomed in closer. "If you look closely, he does have a distinctive tattoo on his lower right arm just above the inner side of his wrist. This surprised me ... this guy has a boot full of arms.

"Great work. Send me all the images and I'll run them through the system," the detective said.

Returning to his desk Detective Adams opened his inbox to reveal the most recent email from Forensic Pathologist, Dr Green.

Home Invasion – 37 Pringle Street, Northbridge

The prints taken from the crime scene were a match for a Gavin Evans. The same Gavin Evans identified as a subject in the Belltrees bunker experiment.

Female Caucasian – Natalie Webb, 25 years

Cause of death – small calibre gunshot wound to the forehead.

Mobile phone found at the crime scene owned by the victim – prints belong to the victim.

Small bag of marijuana – print smudge tested, unable to definitively identify.

Other items found in the victim's handbag revealed victim's prints only.

White card – no prints identified

Blank on one side. On the flipside is a sequence of numbers. Too long to be a phone number or a bank account number. Waiting on expert analysis report.

The detective replied to Dr Green's email thanking him and asking that the prints taken from 73 Pringle Street, Northbridge be fast tracked as he believed all three above cases were linked.

CHAPTER

30

The room was a buzz of chatter when Commander Morgan and Detective Adams entered the meeting room.

The commander stood at the front and welcomed them all. "Good morning. Let's get started. Where are we with the mistaken identity incident at 37 Pringle Street, Northbridge?"

Standing, Detective Adams announced "prints taken from the crime scene were a match for a Gavin Evans. This is the same Gavin Evans identified as a subject in the Belltrees bunker experiment."

All present in the room instantly ceased their chatter and focused on the detective standing in front of them.

Continuing he said, "I have requested a meeting with the taskforce detectives who worked on the Belltrees Incident case. I have also put in a request to have access to the case file notes."

"Ok, let's have an update on the body found near the Wakehurst golf course."

Detective Taylor rose. "As we advised earlier, the female body found with a gunshot wound to the head has been identified as Natalie Webb. Prints taken at the site have identified Perry King, AKA PK, as a person of interest in her murder. Digital Forensics have decoding data written on the white card found on Natalie Webb's body."

The growing chatter in the room didn't stop the detective from continuing.

"Natalie's mother was able to give us a clue for the password on her phone: a childhood named Spud. This password was correct, and Forensics were able to recover data from the phone SIM card retrieved from the crime scene albeit smashed. The last phone call made was to a person named David. One voice message left has also been retrieved."

She pushed the play button. "David, I'm scared. PK attacked me. I passed out and when I woke I found that we were parked in bushland. I heard him talking to you on the phone. I'm hiding in bushland. Someone is coming.""

The recording ended there.

"Also, as I said, the sequence of numbers written on a white card found on Natalie Webb's body has been decoded. Our expert analysist ran a variety of algorithms.

At first nothing made sense and then this popped up. Below are the numbers as presented on the card. The text under is the result of the decoding. Very cleverly written, reading backwards it reads – Benjamin White!"

515423225   4342331152435121

ETIHW   NIMAJNEB

CHAPTER

31

Back at Stephen's house, David opened the trapdoor and heard muffled sounds from within.

"You say something PK?" he asked, roughly removing the gag.

"It's about bloody fucking time!" PK yelled at him. "Where is Stephen?

David pushed an opened bottle of water towards PK's mouth. "Here, drink this."

After a few mouthfuls, PK returned to yelling. "Where is Stephen? What's going to happen to me?"

Replacing the water bottle with the gag, David shoved it into his mouth and barked back, "I don't know. Shut the fuck up, we gotta go!"

It was 10am and David noticed a black SUV with tinted windows parked outside Stephen's house. Pushing PK towards the car, two men jumped out of the black SUV and rushed towards them.

Removing PK's gag one of the men asked, "you PK?"

"Nah, that's him," PK said, pointing at David.

"This is for Eddie," the man said, pistol whipping David as he pushed him on the backseat.

Scumbag! David thought. *You would probably throw your mother under a bus to save yourself!*

Once everyone was inside the vehicle, the men proceeded to drive out of the city.

Looking at the driver, the front passenger confirmed they had come to a good spot and the vehicle came to a stop. Opening the back door, the front passenger pulled David out. He aimed a gun in David's direction and fired one shot.

PK looked frazzled and confused as to what had just happened. Unaware that a recording device was installed in the car PK asked, "you're not going to kill me, are you?"

Trying to make PK think he was important the man said, "the boss has a job for you. We will drop you off at my place to freshen up and then we'll take you to the meeting."

PK began to relax and even started cracking jokes as they headed towards a property in Dural.

"Ok, we're here" the driver announced.

Entering the house PK said, "nice pad mate."

The man pointed to the right. "Bedroom is on the right. There is a change of clothes in the wardrobe. You have thirty minutes before we need to leave."

Showered and dressed PK was feeling quite chuffed with himself as he looked in the mirror. *You're a handsome bastard!*

Leaving the bedroom and walking towards the kitchen he looked around and asked, "I'm starving. Any food in the fridge?"

"Yeah, help yourself," the bodyguard replied.

"Where is your partner?" PK asked.

"Heard a noise outside. Probably a cat looking for a feed, but he's making sure it's nothing to worry about."

"Good job, I'll let the boss know you did your job keeping me safe. Oh, by the way how do I look?"

Disinterested, but not wanting to blow his cover he replied, "great man, the boss is going to love you!"

It was just before 2pm when there was a knock at the door.

The bodyguard moved the curtain and carefully looked through the window. "Fuck! Go into the bedroom and close the door."

PK did as instructed and retreated to the bedroom, keeping the door slightly ajar. He watched and listened through the gap.

The front door suddenly burst open.

"Police! Don't move!" A uniformed police officer yelled out as he pushed his way inside.

Cracking open the door a bit further, PK saw the police walk into the house. "Police! Don't move! Police! Don't move!"

One of the officers saw the bedroom door was slightly ajar. The officer repeated, "this is the police. Put your hands on your head and walk out slowly."

There was no movement from inside the room. The officer repeated, "this is the police. Put your hands on your head and walk out slowly."

PK looked around the room and realised there was no escape. "I am unarmed." PK called as he slowly walked through the doorway.

"I said hands on your head!" the officer yelled pushing PK against the wall.

A shaken PK did as instructed, and the officer pulled each hand to behind his back, placing hand cuffs on his wrists. "Perry King, you are under arrest for the murder of Natalie Webb and Eddie Potts. I caution you that you do not have to say or do anything, but if you do, it may be used in evidence against you."

Feeling dejected, PK lowered his head as he was escorted outside into the police vehicle and transported to the Police station.

Meanwhile, David messaged Benjamin: *job done!*

CHAPTER

32

"Morning Detectives," Adams hollered as he saw Spencer and Walker enter the police taskforce building.

Smiling, Detective Walker introduced his partner, "Detective Spencer, this is my former partner Detective Adams."

"You're both in early," Adams said as he followed them from the lift to the briefing room.

Once sitting Adams said, "so, I hear you are going to interview Perry King."

Both detectives nodded.

"Ok, you both have a copy of the brief, let's go over it together."

Commander Morgan entered the briefing room. All three detectives stood as he entered. "Please sit. I have information pertinent to this meeting today."

"As you will see from the brief, there were two men picked up yesterday. One was Mr Perry King, also known as PK and the other is one of our own who is working undercover. He was instrumental in Perry King's arrest. Mr King believes his friend who was removed from the car was killed with a single gunshot. If he questions you about his friend, known as David, you know nothing."

Detective Adams acknowledged both detectives as they entered Interview Room 1.

PK was sitting quietly as Detective Walker placed a tape in the recorder and said, "the time is 11:05am. My name is Detective Walker and with me is Detective Spencer." Good morning, Mr King. Or do you prefer PK?"

"Why am I here? What did you do to my friend?" PK asked.

Ignoring his questions, Detective Walker placed the audio recorder on the table and said, "Mr King, we'll be asking the questions."

"What is the connection between you and Natalie Webb?" Detective Walker asked.

"Who? I don't know a Natalie Webb."

The detective opened a file, removed a photo and angrily pushed I across the table. "We both know that's not true, don't we Mr King?"

"Oh, you mean Nat? That photo must have been taken a *long* time ago because I haven't seen her for years."

Detective Spencer leaned his arms on the table. "That's interesting as your DNA was found at the crime scene where Natalie Webb's body was found!"

Detective Spencer put two evidence bags on the table, each containing a mobile phone. Touching the first bag he said, "this is Natalie Webb's phone."

Touching the second bag he continued, "this is the SIM card that was removed from Natalie's mobile. The last call has been retrieved. Natalie left an interesting voicemail."

PK's demeanour immediately changes as soon as the recording began.

"Now let's try this again, what is the connection between you and Natalie Webb?" Detective Walker asked.

"I did a few jobs for Eddie Potts. Nat was always at his place, like his girl. We started hanging out together, you know, we smoked some pot, and we became friends. Eddie started giving Nat some coke and she changed - I never do coke - she was always looking for a fix."

"Did you blame Eddie Potts for Miss Webb's behavioural change? Is that why you killed him?" Detective Spencer asked.

"I didn't kill Eddie!"

Detective Walker stood and walked around the table, leaning in close enough to PK that he could feel his hairs stand on end. "How do you explain your DNA being found on the murder weapon at Eddie Pott's house?"

PK placed his hands over his forehead before blurting out, "Eddie and I had an agreement. He would steal the shipment from Benjamin White. Eddie paid me with coke, and I would off-sell some of it to my customers. I heard he was going to cut me out of the shipment!"

"Now, that wasn't too difficult!" Detective Spencer said before terminating the interview and pressed stop on the recording device. Then, both Detectives left the room.

CHAPTER

33

The commander had arrived at the rendezvous when David walked in via the back entrance of the bookshop.

"This must be urgent. You've never sounded so spooked," the commander said.

David retrieved a file from his backpack and placed it on the table.

"This is the file I showed you at our last meeting. As you saw before there is no photo ID." He placed a photo on the table. "This is a photo of Henry White."

"Now, I checked the national database using the name and date of birth Benjamin gave me, this is the mugshot I found." He placed another photo beside the first photo. "The question is, does Benjamin know he has a half-brother?"

"Did he give you any indication that he may have met this man?" the commander asked.

"None at all. I received a phone call from the desk sergeant at Belrose Police Station. He told me a man attended to report his friend was missing. Alarm bells rang for the sergeant when this man who initially had an English accent suddenly reverted to an Australian accent as he appeared to get frustrated with the questioning. The desk sergeant sent across the recording of the interview. I didn't see it at first, but as the interview went on, there was something about the man that played on my mind. I decided to check and see if Benjamin White had ever been interviewed. My suspicions were correct. He reported a break-in earlier in the year. It appears unrelated to what we are working on now, but it was his mannerism and quick frustrated responses to questions that made me curious. It turns out the friend he was reporting missing was in fact, Perry King AKA KP. This is the same man that you delivered to the safe house earlier in the week."

"What did you tell Benjamin about what you did with PK?

"I haven't told him anything, now it looks like I should have."

"Well, I've covered for you this time, but this can't happen again, you understand. You're supposed to be out of the picture, I asked the boys to set a scene as if PK took an overdose. Here are a couple of photos for you to keep. They'll show that you found PK dead after using. You drove out to Mittagong and left his body in a car just off the Hume Highway."

Taking out his notebook the commander continued, "I made a few phone calls and found out that former ASIO Agent Allan has had two visitors only, his wife and Robert Burns."

CHAPTER

34

"Good afternoon, I'm Fiona Forrester, coming to you live from News Central Radio 101. Welcome to Midday! Wasn't it a beautiful weekend! Slightly cooler mornings but the days are gorgeous. Autumn is my favourite season. Top temperature today for both Sydney and the western suburbs will be 26 degrees with an overnight low of 16 degrees.

"Local artist Wendy James will be dropping in this afternoon.

"Rugby league season has started. John Thomas will be giving his insight into the footy season.

"Breaking news just in: Arrest made in relation to a woman's body found near the Wakehurst Golf Course and the body of a man found in a house in Northbridge. Channel 9 reporter Lee Baker is on the line with an update. Lee, what are Police saying about the arrest?"

"Fiona, in a police press conference this morning it was stated that a man has been taken in for questioning over the deaths of twenty-eight-year-old Natalie Webb whose body was found near the Wakehurst Golf Course and Eddie Potts, a small time drug dealer from Northbridge.

Police have not advised whether all three were known to each other."

"Thank you, Lee.

"My first guest this afternoon, Wendy James has just walked into the studio and has brought in a few of her pieces of artwork. Welcome Wendy. We have met before but for our listeners, tell us a little bit about yourself."

"I'm a 41-year-old happily married mum of three beautiful but crazy kids.

I work from home and juggle all the things that life with three kids throws at me."

"What does your artwork represent?"

"The style of art I enjoy is called Acrylic pouring, being so abstract it can represent different feelings or moods which can be expressed through the different colours I use or the technique. There are many different techniques that can be used for pour painting depending on the style or effect you're wanting to achieve."

"What inspires you?"

"My biggest inspiration to paint is the fact that this is something that I do just for me. Being so busy and doing so much for the family, I really wanted something that was just mine. The reason I got into acrylic pouring was really from watching endless videos on YouTube which I found very therapeutic. It's amazing how much time can pass when you get mesmerised by watching people create such beautiful pieces."

"What does your artwork mean to you?"

"Being in the zone and creating something beautiful, when most of the time I really have no expectations, can be quite therapeutic and calming. I can be quite limited with the time I get to spend painting, so I really do cherish that time and let my creative juices flow."

"Great to see you again Wendy. Anyone that is interested in seeing Wendy's artwork, her details will be posted on News Central Radio 101 website.

"John Thomas is on the line to give his insight of the footy season."

Thank-you Fiona. Let's begin with the ARL lineup which starts this weekend. The transfer of players has narrowed the gap between the weaker sides and holds for a great season.

"The AFL season has commenced, and it looks like the leading teams will dominate this year's competition again.

"Soccer season is half over, two of the Victorian teams breaking away on the table.

"It's also very exciting to see Australian Cricket healthier than ever in both the men's and women's competitions.

"That's a wrap from me. Back to you Fiona."

"Thanks John. The lines are open listeners, give me a call now on 131101."

CHAPTER

35

Benjamin was surprised when David messaged him saying to let him know he had found out something about Robert Burns.

"Meet me at Hews Court just down the road from the pub in Belrose at midday," Benjamin excitedly replied.

David parked behind Benjamin's vehicle. He picked up the paperwork and exited his car, quickly hopping in the front of the vehicle.

"I drove out to the address on the file you gave me. It looked like an old, abandoned factory. At first there was no movement, but there was a black SUV ute with an open cargo area was parked adjacent to a side door. This vehicle looked like the SUV that Stephen and I saw at Pyrmont. As I was about to throw in the towel, three men dressed in black overalls and wearing beanies that resembled rolled up balaclavas exited from a rear door and got into the same vehicle" he said.

Opening the file David laid down two photos he had taken. Pointing to the first photo he said, "this man then exited that same door. He was walking with a fairly sedate looking girl."

Pointing to the second photo he continued, "you can see she was hooked up to some sort of a leash like the kind you would put on a dog. He walked her to the black SUV and placed her inside securing her lead to the seat."

"Fuck! That's Susan!"

"The question remains is, is this the same group that broke into Henry's home, left the ransom note and arranged for the SUV to drive to the deserted building at Pyrmont?"

Benjamin didn't know how much Stephen had told David and began to give him the run down on the bunker fire and what had followed.

"I'm not sure if you heard about the fire in the old WWII bunker at Belltrees late last year. There were two AI's that Henry and I had been training to be part of our arsenal, you know-weapons we could use at jobs. One named Gavin followed commands to a tee chasing down anything that moved. The second was named Susan. That's who you saw at Pyrmont. Susan initially followed instructions but then she became hesitant. She started doing the opposite of the commands given, as if she was making up her own mind."

"I had been working with them in a huge empty factory lot. Finishing up for the day, I gave the command for both Gavin and Susan to return to me but only Gavin came back. When I searched the spot where I had last seen Susan, there was a black signal box lying in the grass. Henry gave me a serve; told me I was becoming sloppy. He even suggested that I may have been followed." "An IT guru acquaintance of mine examined the black signal box and told me that it could have been used to interfere with my commands."

Scratching his head, Benjamin continued, "this was around the same time that a rival establishment approached me saying they wanted to buy Susan. I told them she wasn't for sale. We found Susan wandering around the back of the factory lot and Henry took her back to his house. I told Henry I would keep Gavin with me at my house."

Raising a finger to interrupt the conversation David said, "I found out a couple of things about Robert Burns. First, he isn't on social media, and the second, is he has visited Agent Allan in prison. I got in touch with a couple of buddies of mine, showed them the photos and asked if they could ask around."

Benjamin raised his eyebrows as he asked, "exactly who are your buddies?"

"Let's say buddies that turn a blind eye to my own business dealings, and I keep their bribes a secret!" Continuing he asked, "do you have any siblings?"

Benjamin replied, "Henry adopted me when I was three. It was always just the two of us."

"Well, this is going to knock your socks off. Robert Burns is in the police database, but where it gets interesting is, he was born Trevor White. He's the son of Henry White!"

CHAPTER

36

David sat in the dog park watching the dogs and their humans interacting when he felt a little nudge and heard a whimpering sound from Sacha.

"Woof back at you," he said stroking her fur. As he began the walk home he reminded her, "Don't get too used to me."

Benjamin was leaning on his front fence. He kept looking at his phone and then looking up to the sky, shaking his head. Not you again.

Benjamin spotted him and with a grin on his face said, "the two of you look good together!" I'm going to go and confront Henry about Trevor and seeing as it was you that retrieved the info thought you should come with me."

"Look, this is family business. I don't want to get caught up in your family woes," David replied.

"I'll pretend I didn't hear that. Now, while you put your little pet away, I'll phone Henry and tell him we want to meet up and we are on our way."

As David exited his house Benjamin said, "it's all set."

As they drove through Redfern, David looked intently at the urban blight, disappointed that parts of Redfern remained in urban decline.

The old storage warehouse came into sight with only a few cars parked in the street. In its day David thought this block would have been the business hub of the area, built before the boom but all that remained now were vandalised storage lots, some crawling with rats and other vermin.

Henry's bodyguard was standing next to the car, hands folded in front. He turned slightly as he opened the vehicle door announcing that Benjamin had arrived.

Exiting his car Henry asked, "what's this about?"

Looking at him David interjected, "I found out something interesting about Robert Burns."

Without looking at David and sounding very irritated henry replied, "I'm not asking you."

Benjamin jumped in, "he found a rival business that is trying to move into our territory. Coincidentally this is run by a Robert Burns". What I found the most intriguing is that Robert Burns is your son Trevor White!" Benjamin stepped forward and pointing his finger accusingly at Henry. "You adopted me at age four and all this time you never told me you had a son, or that I had a brother. What sort of father does that?"

"There is a lot you don't know son. Back in the 1993, your uncle Alex kidnapped a young woman in South Australia and began experimenting on her. She died, but there was a complication. She had a three-year-old son named Benjamin. I couldn't stop thinking about what would happen to you, so I adopted you. Trevor was always a disappointment to me. It was your uncle's idea that he change his name to Robert Burns and start a new life. We offered to give our contacts to him, but he was determined to make it on his own. He made it clear that didn't need our help."

"Everything was going according to plan until the ASIO Agent, Brian Allan, got involved and he got his daughter into the bunker. You know the rest of the story and how that panned out."

"Well seeing as you have brought up Agent Allan, here is something that will be of interest to you. Robert Burns has visited Agent Allan in jail." And with that, Benjamin stormed away from the car.

CHAPTER

37

Trevor White pulled up outside the exclusive Belrose house that Benjamin White resided in. *Fuck you Dad! You certainly treat your adopted son with respect.* He walked up the pathway to the front door, inconspicuously looking through one of the front windows.

Benjamin came around from the side of the house. "What the fuck do you want?"

Trevor extended his hand to shake and formally announced himself.

Benjamin pushed his hand aside and again repeated, "what the fuck do you want?"

"Let me introduce myself."

"I know who you are! You have a nerve coming to my place!"

Changing the subject Trevor commented, "nice place you have here. You must be doing ok for yourself to drive a Mercedes."

"We both know you're not here to admire my place or my car. Tell me one good reason why I shouldn't call the police and report a trespasser on my property?"

"Go ahead! I'm sure the police would be interested to learn of the activities you and Henry have been doing of late. Or we could have a chat here."

"So what do I call you? Robert Burns or Trevor White?" Benjamin sarcastically asked.

Ignoring the question Trevor replied, "you certainly have our Pop's disposition don't you Ben, or do you prefer to be called Benjamin?"

"You don't know anything at all about me."

"Oh, but I do. Your real name was Benjamin Hanson. My father adopted you after your poor mummy disappeared. How am I going so far?"

"A part of me wants to punish both you because he chose you over me. I was never good enough. He always criticised me and kept telling me how he now had the son that could control and grow the business."

"I first met Agent Allan two years ago. He knew me as Robert Burns. At first, I didn't know what he was working on but then he told me about his involvement with the Belltrees bunker experiment, working with a scientist and doctor, Dr Alex Marinov and Henry White."

Taking a photo from his jacket pocket and handing it to Benjamin, Trevor pointed to each man as he named them. "Dr Marinov, Henry White and then there's you. Benjamin White, Henry's adopted son. I saw something in that photo that I have never had, a father's love.

"I did a few small jobs for Agent Allan. One day he phoned me saying it was time that I met Henry. I messaged him at the last minute saying I couldn't make it. Agent Allan must have had a falling out with Henry because when I eventually told him my real name, he suggested we work together. Revenge sounded so much more attractive to me than being known as the unwanted son. I wanted to prove to him that I was worthy.

"At first, I was hesitant. What if my father found out that I was working with Agent Allan? Then I thought, no I am going to prove him wrong.

"When the Government canned the bunker experiments, Dr Marinov said he wasn't interested in experimenting on Susan. Agent Allan informed me that they needed a diversion, hence the bunker fire.

"I made it my goal to take everything from him, including both Gavin and Susan. Agent Allan sent me a letter. I read it over and over trying to understand what it meant, then I got it; he wanted me to check in on Henry and the two assets, Susan, and Gavin. From that day I have been visiting Agent Allan in prison and together we have been working on a plan for me to take over the business. Just think if we could sell both Susan and Gavin to overseas interests, we would be millionaires."

Before he could utter another word, Benjamin angrily butted in and said, "you broke into Henry's place and trashed it, and left the ransom note. I suppose it was you who also organised the 'so-called' meeting at Pyrmont. But Susan wasn't sitting in the back of the SUV. It was all a hoax. I know it was you who took Gavin!"

"We are on the same side here Benjamin. My father, our father is losing it!"

"That's where you are wrong. Read my lips, go fuck yourself!"

Talking out loud to himself he said, "Hi Trish, check in on Henrietta and tell me how the kids are going."

CHAPTER

38

When he met up with Henry and Benjamin, Dan said "with everything that has been going on lately, I touched base with a couple of my old buddies. They told me there was an uncover cop working with Stephen. He goes by the name of David Prentice."

Benjamin jumped in and said, "Stephen first introduced me to David at his place. Apparently, David had done a couple of jobs for him. He told me that he was trustworthy."

"Did you check him out?" Dan queried.

Benjamin looked down at the ground silently when Henry yelled, "well did you check him out?"

"No, I didn't. Stephen told me he had been inside, small time stuff. He followed David one day and saw what David did to two thugs trying to rob a convenience store. Apparently, he covered his face before marching into the store and bashed the crap out of the thugs. Crouching down he stuffed some of the money in his pocket before proceeding to hand the rest to the worker and leaving the store. He was cool and didn't create any suspicion by hiding his deception."

"Fuck son! That's a good story, but I've told you that before you bring anyone into the business do a thorough background check," Henry sharply retorted.

"I Thought I would let Stephen go; he was becoming unreliable."

"Where is Stephen now?" Dan asked.

"Dead!"

"I hope you didn't use this place to interview David?" Henry asked.

"Yes, but I took precautions. Stephen used the limo. He knew the instructions; he was required to have a hood on his head."

Henry shook his head and rolled his eyes.

Feeling under pressure Benjamin then sharply said, "the hood was removed from David's head once they securely entered the underground parking area. I was angry at Stephen, so I shot him. David took the phone; he knew that this was his only method of communication. Ralph put a hood on David's head before driving him back to the city. He dropped him off at Central.

"David's first job was to get rid of PK. He messaged me once the job was done. I've been using him ever since.

He gave me no reason to believe he wasn't who he said he was. I met him in an alley behind his local. He was the one who told me about Robert … or should I say Trevor?"

A ding sounded on his phone. Checking the text Benjamin said, "speaking of Trevor, he just sent a message saying he has Susan, and they are at the old weatherboard house at Seven Hills."

Henry turned away from Benjamin as he said to Dan, "I want to know everything about David Prentice, where he goes and who he sees!"

"Already done sir. At this very moment, my men are watching him walk a dog at the park near his home. They are waiting for your instructions." Dan replied.

"Get him and secure him at the house!" Henry yelled.

CHAPTER

39

"Lots of smells today Sacha," David said as he bent down and patted her head.

As his eyes reached the street level, he noticed there were more than the usual dog walkers in the park as he began to profile what he called 'stiff walkers'.

Suddenly an entourage of men started menacingly walking towards him. Removing the mobile phone from the top pocket of his shirt he sent a text to the commander; *cover blown, one hundred seconds to midnight,* before rubbing his right wrist and quietly whispering, "please find me" as he threw away the phone.

At the edge of the park, he caught a glimpse of his neighbour and called out, "hey Dorothy, lovely day for a walk."

As she bent down and patted Sacha on her head he asked, "can I ask you for a big favour Dorothy? Work just phoned. I need to go to the office. Can you take Sacha home with you? I'll come and get her once I get home."

Dorothy was always happy to look after Sacha but was astounded to see the leash on the ground and David nowhere to be seen.

The commander was sitting at his desk when he saw the text message from David.

"Martin, do you have a minute?" he called out as he opened his office door looking in Martin's direction. Please come in and close the door behind you. What I am about to tell you is classified information and must be kept between us. Can I trust you?"

"Absolutely sir."

"As you know, we have an undercover police officer working on the Belltrees bunker case. His undercover name is David. For security reasons his real name can never be revealed.

"There is a code that he uses only if he felt his cover had been compromised. I just received this text from him." He passed his mobile to the detective.

Detective Adams looked at him with his head tilted to one side and said,

"Cover blown, one hundred seconds to midnight."

"He has a RFID tag implanted on his wrist which is being tracked by a device inserted in my mobile phone. If for any reason he felt that his cover was blown, he would send me this text message so I could track the tag device. Hence, one hundred seconds to midnight.

"Take this phone and get your best IT technician on this now. We need to know David's exact location. Also, we need everyone working on the Belltrees taskforce in the meeting room now. This takes priority over anything they are presently working on."

"I'm on it sir."

Martin walked into the IT department and approached Russell's desk. He passed him the phone and said, "using this I need you find the location of the GPS tracker. Whatever you are working on now, this has top priority. Oh, and by the way this is strictly between you and me."

"Yep, got it. This won't take long if you want to wait," Russell replied.

Russell used the mobile phone to remotely access the device. He quickly brought it up on the monitor. "Ok, looks like this phone is tracking an RFID tag."

"Can you connect my mobile so I can also see the location of the tag and monitor its movements?" Martin asked.

"That's a bit trickier. It may take me about ten minutes."

Leaving his mobile with Russell he said, "great, "I'll be in the taskforce meeting room. I expect to see you in precisely 10 minutes" he confirmed as he left the IT department.

"Great. I'll be in the taskforce meeting room. I expect to see you in precisely ten minutes," Martin confirmed as he left the IT department.

Detective Adams gave the commander the nod as he walked into the taskforce meeting room.

"Good afternoon everyone. Thank you all for making yourself available at such short notice. There has been a development in the Belltrees bunker case. I recently informed you all that one of our own was working undercover. About an hour ago I received a text message from him advising that his cover had been compromised," the commander said.

Martin felt a firm tap on his shoulder and Russell had entered the meeting room.

"All done! Here is your mobile with the tracking on it as you requested. This room has an electronic whiteboard so the team viewer app I installed will allow you to share your phone screen. It's all set up, just press share with the whiteboard to reveal the map."

The commander then asked, "Detective Adams do you have an update for us please?"

Looking at Russell, Detective Adams stood up as he said, "thank you. Please stay here in case I need you regarding the map."

Martin walked over to the commander and returned his mobile phone. He then continued to the front of the room, pressing "share" to enable the map on his own phone to appear on the whiteboard.

"As the commander just told us, about an hour ago he received a text message from David, the officer working undercover, advising that his cover had been blown. He activated the implanted tracking device."

The room went quiet. Using the walkie talkie, the detective contacted the Strike Force Commander.

"Commander this is Detective Adams from the Taskforce Headquarters. We have been tracking an RFID tag of an undercover officer who has been taken hostage, travelling in a vehicle heading in a westerly direction towards Parramatta Jail. This vehicle has now been stationary for five minutes, location is the corner of O'Connell and Dunlop Streets, Parramatta."

"Detectives Walker and Spencer will meet you there."

"This is Strike Force Commander Thompson. Copy that. We are currently on route to the location."

Returning his focus to the group in the room, he pointed to the map.

"This dot is David's current position. The second dot is the Strike Force location."

The room went quiet, like a graveyard at midnight!

CHAPTER

40

Detective Adams pressed the transmit mode button and asked, "Commander, what is your present location?"

The response came quickly, "this is Strike Force Commander Thompson. We are currently on O'Connell Street heading in a westerly direction to the rendezvous location. ETA approximately one minute."

Keeping the radio frequency open, Strike Force Commander Thompson then said, "arrived at location. Police have already established a two-hundred metre exclusion zone around the disused weatherboard house. Passing a photo to his men he added, "this is the undercover officer taken hostage."

Back at headquarters, the police taskforce room was buzzing with the conversation between the Strike Force Commander and both Detectives Walker and Spencer.

Speaking into his walkie talkie Detective Adams said, "Commander Thompson, I have just sent you photos of Henry White, Benjamin White and Robert Burns."

"Thank you, Detective," the commander replied, forwarding the photos to his men. Giving designated orders to his team the commander said, "Taylor, Henderson, and Smith, check around the back of the building to see if there is an exit door. Brown, Lee, and I will remain in the front."

"Commander, there is no back door. Stairs lead to a second-floor covered veranda type room. We have climbed the stairs and will wait for your instructions," Taylor said.

"Copy that," the commander replied. The commander looked at the Detectives. "We will enter the premises. Remain here until I give the all clear that it is safe for you to enter."

Both men nodded in agreement.

"Go! Go! Go!" the commander yelled.

Breaking down both upstairs and downstairs doors to gain entry, the commander and his team yelled, "Police, don't move!" as they forced their way into the old house.

Upstairs, coming from behind a half wall room divider, an armed man wielding with what appeared to be a semi-automatic firearm ran towards Taylor. Taylor was able to dodge a bullet before pulling her own trigger and hitting the man once in the chest. As the man fell to the ground, he lost hold of his firearm allowing Taylor to safely kick it aside.

At the same time, also upstairs, an unarmed perpetrator ran towards one of the team.

"Get down on the ground and put your hands behind your head!" Smith yelled, pushing the man to the floor. Once he was secure, Smith handcuffed him. He walked him out of the building and down the stairs into a police van.

"Shot fired! Returned fire, perpetrator down," Taylor announced.

Downstairs was deserted apart from a figure sitting on a chair with his back facing the officers and with a black hood over his head.

"Don't shoot!" a male voice cried out.

Approaching the man, Brown announced, "I am going to remove the hood. Remain very still. Do you understand?"

"Yes, understood," the male voice replied.

Removing the hood, Brown asked, "what is your name?"

"My name is David Prentice. I am a police officer working undercover. My captors didn't think to check my pockets. You will find my ID in my back left-hand there!"

After confirming the captive man was indeed David Prentice, Brown untied him and offered him a drink of water.

"David, I'm Strike Force Commander Thompson. We have overpowered and disabled two captors upstairs. I know you had a hood over your head, how many captors do you believe were downstairs with you?"

Closing his eyes as if to return to his hooded state, he moved his head to the right before opening his eyes and saying, "I heard footsteps walking above me. I also heard what sounded like a trapdoor being closed and bolted down in the right-hand corner of the room."

Putting a finger on his lips and using his other hand he pointed as he whispered for David to retreat to the left side of the room.

Looking back at his officers, the commander put two fingers to his eyes and pointed to the right side of the room giving the order for his men to check for a trapdoor.

After hearing the conversation between David Prentice and the Commander, Taylor returned with bolt cutters.

With Brown assisting, the commander walked to the right side of the room and cut the bolt. He slowly opening the trapdoor. From what he could see, there were a set of stairs and what looked like a tunnel heading off to the right.

"Brown, Taylor, and Smith, check the trapdoor and see where the tunnel leads. Henderson and Lee will stay here with David and myself."

Walking to the entrance door the commander said, "Detectives Walker and Spencer, it is now safe for you to enter the building."

Once inside both detectives introduced themselves to David and asked if he was up to giving a few details of what had happened.

After taking a brief statement from David, Detective Walker said that there was an ambulance at the furthest end of the exclusion zone. He then suggested David allow the ambulance officers to check him over.

Once David was safely in the ambulance, Detectives Walker and Spencer returned to the Strike Force Leader who was standing with his men on the adjacent footpath.

"Commander, we have walked approximately fifty metres and to the end of the tunnel. There are stairs leading up to what we believe would be ground level, but it appears that the opening has been locked from the outside," Taylor said.

"Roger that. Make your way back to the house," the commander replied.

The Strike Force team were packing up their gear when suddenly a strange figure wearing a thick heavy hiking jacket appeared from the bushes near where Taylor had said the tunnel ended.

Detective Spencer moved forward, removing his glock from its holster. "Stop right there and put your hands on your head!"

At that very moment, all officers looked in the direction of what appeared to be a teenage girl. They were busy arming themselves with their weapons and hadn't realised what they were seeing until Detective Walker said, "wait, its Susan!"

CHAPTER

41

Detective Walker took a step forward towards Susan when the Strike Force Commander called out to him, "Detective, you need to listen to me! Pay careful attention to what I am saying. We don't know if she has a weapon under that jacket."

Without taking his eyes off the girl Detective Walker replied, "I met Susan at Port Macquarie Hospital and we had a connection. I'm going to talk to her and see I can get her to sit on the ground."

"Taylor, Smith and Brown, see if you can work your way round and get behind her," the commander ordered.

Once all three officers were in place, Detective Walker took a step forward. Susan started tilting her head from side to side.

"Commander, can your men widen their perimeter? I could be wrong, but I think there is someone hiding in the bushes controlling her" Walker said.

He took another step forward and said, "Hello Susan, I'm Detective Walker. Do you remember when I visited you in the hospital?"

Replying in a deeper voice than he remembered, Susan said, "that's close enough!"

"Do you remember me? I'm the policeman from the underground house. I visited you in the hospital."

Looking straight at the detective, Susan asked "Dr Alex is my friend. Did he come with you?"

Detective Walker was pleased that some of her memories were still embedded in her brain.

He thought it best not to tell Susan that Dr Marinov was deceased, especially if he wanted to keep her calm. "No, I'm sorry he didn't come with me."

It appeared that Susan was having a traumatic brain injury episode. She began moving her head quickly from side to side, starting to lose her balance when she suddenly stopped. "You said you would try and visit me again in the hospital, but you never came back."

"I'm sorry Susan, but I'm here now."

Moving slowly, he took a small bar of chocolate from his shirt pocket and asked, "would you like some chocolate?"

Returning from the bushes, Officer Smith said, "Commander we have one perpetrator in custody. Henry

White. Two men identified as Benjamin White and Trevor White have escaped, and both may be heading in your direction. They will be coming in from the left side of your position."

Suddenly two men, one armed with a semi-automatic firearm emerged from the bushes and approached Susan and the detective. Benjamin pushed Trevor towards the detective. "Get over there Robert, Trevor or whatever you call yourself!"

Showing no fear Detective Walker said, "Benjamin, I know you believe Dr Marinov was a monster for experimenting on your mother. I listened to some of the cassettes from his journals. Did you know that it was Henry and *not* Dr Marinov who experimented on your mother? He described in detail how he tortured her."

Trevor jumping in, further tormenting Benjamin. "I told you my father is evil. He killed your poor mummy. Did he adopt you out of guilt? Probably!"

Benjamin pointed his weapon, switching direction between Detective Walker and Trevor. Susan suddenly moved. She stood with outstretched arms in front of both men as if to protect them. With a pleading voice she called out, "no Benjamin!"

"You are useless to me!" he yelled back before pulling the trigger. The bullet hit Susan in the chest, and she fell to the ground.

There was no way out for him now. Realising this, he placed the firearm under his chin and pulled the trigger one final time.

THE END